IN A MIST

IN A MIST

DEVON CODE

Invisible Publishing
Halifax & Montréal

Text copyright © Devon Code, 2007

All rights reserved. No part of this publication may be reproduced or transmitted in any form, by any method, without the prior written consent of the publisher.

Some of the stories in this collection have been previously published.

Alice and Roy originally appeared in Invisible Publishing's Transits Anthology; Edgar and Morty appeared in the Soul Gazers Anthology; The White Knight was short-listed for the 2007 Aeon Award in Albedo 1 Magazine (UK) and Aricia Agestis appeared in print and online in Neon Literary Magazine (UK).

Library and Archives Canada Cataloguing in Publication

Code, Devon, 1981-
    In a mist / Devon Code.

ISBN 978-0-9782185-3-9

    I. Title.

PS8605.O32I55 2007   C813'.6   C2007-905207-X

Cover Design & Typesetting by Megan Fildes

Printed and bound in Canada

Invisible Publishing
Halifax & Montréal
www.invisiblepublishing.com

For Mary Code

July, 1978	1
Alice and Roy	11
Edgar and Morty	25
The Death of Benjamin Hirsch	41
The White Knight	53
The Flank and Spur	63
The Crow's Nest	79
June, 1978	95
Aricia Agestis	101

July, 1978

When Herb came home that afternoon there was no one there. He went into the bedroom to see if Sue was resting and found the covers smoothed neatly over the empty bed. He sat on the corner of the mattress, tried to recall if she had mentioned taking the girls somewhere that afternoon. Then he slipped his suspenders off his shoulders and kicked off his shoes. He took the pint bottle of gin out of his delivery bag, twisted off the cap and drank from it. The gin burned pleasantly as it coursed down his throat. He went into the kitchen and stood in front of the refrigerator. The girls' report cards had been there when he left that morning but now in their place was a note written in his wife's precise hand, held to the refrigerator door with a magnet shaped like a daisy.

We have left. Please don't try to find us. The utilities are paid up until the end of the month. —*Susan*

He set the gin bottle down on the kitchen table and took the note off the refrigerator and held it in his hand, staring at it.

"Jesus Christ," he said. Then he ripped the note in two and threw it in the wastebin in the cupboard under the sink. He went into the girls' room, pulled out the top drawer of the dresser and it fell to the floor, empty. He looked on the bed for Sarah's Raggedy Ann doll and did not find it. Then he looked in the closet. Their summer dresses were all gone, their winter coats, and Melanie's picture books. He went back into his room and looked at the top of Susan's vanity and saw that it was empty. He wrenched out her underwear drawer and all it contained was a beige maternity bra and a crimson teddy he had bought for her on their first anniversary. He looked in the closet, rifling through his shirts and pressed slacks. The only articles of Susan's clothing still there were ones she had not worn in years.

"Christ," he said. "Susan."

He went into the living room, picked up the phone and dialled his sister-in-law's number.

"Hello?" said a woman's voice.

"Where is she, Joan?" said Herb. He heard Joan muffle the receiver and whisper something.

"Herb? That's you isn't it? You've been drinking," said Joan.

"Are they with you?"

He strained to hear the sounds of children's voices but all he could make out in the background was a game show on the television.

"They're not here. If they've gone somewhere I don't know where. Just sit tight and I'm sure they'll turn up. Goodbye, Herb."

"I'm coming over, Joan and you're going to tell me—"

"No, you can't come over Herb. I'm hanging up now. You should wait there in case they come back."

"Joan," yelled Herb. He could hear a man's voice in the

July, 1978

background.

"Hello?" said his brother-in-law, speaking too loudly.

"Lyle, tell me where they are," said Herb. He was shaking. He gripped the arm of the chair in order to steady himself, his thick fingers digging into the soft upholstery.

"Herb, listen, whatever's happened, I'm sure Sue and the girls are fine."

"Don't tell me that," said Herb. "I'm coming over there." Herb could hear the slurring now in his speech and a rage that surprised him.

"I don't think so. How do you plan on getting here? Me and Joan are just sitting down to an early dinner."

"Oh yeah?" said Herb.

"Tell you what, Herb. I'm on night shift, but why don't I come over after dinner and you can tell me what's on your mind?"

"I've got nothing to say to you, Lyle," Herb yelled.

"Be reasonable. You're going to give yourself a heart attack."

Herb slammed the receiver down and then dialled the military hospital.

"How may I direct your call?" said the operator.

"This is an emergency," he said. "Susan McConnell is a night nurse on the fifth floor. She recently applied for a transfer. I need to know where."

"May I ask who's calling please?" said the receptionist.

Herb considered his reply.

"This is her brother-in-law. This is a family emergency," said Herb.

"I'm afraid I don't have that information," said the operator. "If you like I can take down a message and forward—"

Herb slammed down the receiver. He knocked over the end table and the phone fell to the floor.

"Christ!" he screamed. He went back into the kitchen

and took the gin bottle and drank from it as if it were a glass of milk after a rich dessert or a cold beer on a hot day.

Then he went into the living room and sank down on the sofa, the springs creaking under his bulk. He rested the gin bottle on the shag carpet and took the pack of cigarettes from his breast pocket, undid the buttons of his sweat-stained shirt and dropped it on the floor. He took off his glasses, rubbed his temples and closed his eyes. Sitting in the silence and the heat of the empty room he remembered dropping Susan off at the hospital one morning, years ago before she switched to nights and started taking the car. He remembered watching from the car as a young officer in immaculate dress uniform held the door open for her, the way she looked at him in that uniform.

The overturned telephone started to beep in the corner. He opened his eyes, put his glasses back on and struggled to his feet. When he got to the phone he picked it up with both hands and wrenched the cord out of the wall. He held it over his head and launched it across the room. The bell chimed on impact and he could see an indentation behind the beige floral wallpaper. When he turned he saw that he had knocked over the gin bottle, its contents spilling out onto the carpet in a dark puddle.

"Son of a bitch."

He picked up the gin bottle and finished off what remained. He went over to the mantlepiece and put the empty bottle down. The only remaining photograph was from the summer before. The girls, Melanie and Sarah, standing under an oak tree in Canterbury Park, wearing purple and white velour dresses with white stockings and black Mary Janes. In front of them, the Kwong boy from next door, shorter than the girls, grinning, dressed in short pants and a yellow Mickey Mouse t-shirt. The boy seemed always to be riding his tricycle in circles in his driveway.

July, 1978

He would greet Herb enthusiastically as "Mr. McConnell" whenever they met. Herb remembered how the boy's father once found him passed out on the lawn early one morning, and had helped him into the house before Susan got home from work. But when this photograph showed up on the mantlepiece, Herb asked Sue why the Kwong boy was on permanent display in the company of his daughters. Melanie overheard her father and said that Henry looked up to him because he was a postman. Herb told his daughter that the boy was a fool. He turned the picture face down now, picked up his cigarettes and lit one as he went into the kitchen.

He sat at the table and tried to calm his nerves. While he smoked he studied the calendar hanging on the wall. He saw that Sue had written *scrub the floor* under the day's date. He surveyed the brown and white linoleum at his feet but he couldn't tell how clean it was. He went to the refrigerator and found a package of bologna and a carton of milk he did not remember being there when he had left for work that morning. He took them out and put them on the counter along with mayonnaise and a jar of pickles. He poured himself a glass of milk and took a loaf of bread from the breadbox and made two sandwiches and sat down at the table.

When he finished, he took a jar from the refrigerator with a hand-written label that read *Strawberry Jam, August 1977*. He made himself one more sandwich, finishing the jam. As he lit his last cigarette, it occurred to him he might never taste that homemade jam again. He put the plate in the sink and opened the cabinet where they kept the grocery money. He took down the Christmas shortbread tin and he could tell by its weight that it contained no loose change and when he took off the lid he found another note:

July 3rd, $20 credit at Dominion Grocery (Walkley Road).

His temper flared and then abated as he realized he could at least use the credit for cigarettes. He was surprised Sue had not thought of this.

He sat back down sideways on the kitchen chair as he smoked and stared at three earthenware jars on the back of the counter, deep orange with brown lips and lids marked *Flour, Sugar, Salt*, descending in size. Next to the flour jar stood the coffee pot, a General Electric model shaped like an oblong teapot. He remembered that his sister-in-law had bought it on sale at Woolworth's. One for herself and one for Sue. Herb's face looked back at him from the polished chrome surface, distorted, an indistinct blur.

He got up and opened the cupboard under the sink, retrieved the note from the wastebin and lined up the two torn halves on the kitchen table, as if to mend the damage. Then he went to the writing desk in the corner of the living room, searched until he found a roll of Scotch tape in the middle drawer next to a pair of scissors. Beneath the tape was a manila envelope with his wife's name written in a woman's handwriting he did not recognize. He picked it up and inside he found a sheet of white cardboard with cellophane pouches displaying silver coins. There were two rows with five coins in each row: ten pristine effigies of King George the Fifth, one half-dollar for each year from 1921 to 1930. He tried to think of where they had come from exactly and he recalled attending a funeral in Deep River for Sue's aunt, remembered how quiet Sue had been for weeks afterward. He checked his wristwatch and he knew there was no way he'd make it to the pawn shop before it closed.

"Shit."

He left the coin collection on top of the desk and sat back down on the sofa. He had only rested for a minute when he heard the car outside and looked up to see the black Buick pulling into the driveway. He got up and went

July, 1978

to the back door. He moved his old guitar case aside and found his tool box easily without the usual clutter of rubber boots and running shoes for little feet. He chose the forged steel carpenter's hammer and placed his sweaty palm upon its rubber grip just as he heard the rapping on the screen door.

By the time he made it back to the living room, Lyle had let himself in and stood facing him, his considerable frame filling the front doorway: a silhouette against the golden summer light. Herb held the hammer at his side, shielded his eyes and stared at his brother-in-law.

"Doing a bit of handiwork?" said Lyle, as if speaking to a deaf man. The two men stood there for some time, not moving. Herb searched the calm of Lyle's expression and he could find no trace of fear. Then Herb cleared his throat.

"Don't see much point," said Herb finally, tossing the hammer onto the cushion of the chesterfield.

"I'm sure you've had a long day," said Lyle. "Hot day to be carrying mail. Best to take it easy." Herb looked at him without saying anything.

"My day's just starting," said Lyle. "Though I've been up all afternoon. Hard to get any sleep in this damn heat." He took a step forward. "You going to ask me to sit down before I go?"

Herb walked over to the sofa and sat down with a grunt, the hammer shifting as the cushions swelled with his weight.

Lyle took off his driver's cap, bent toward his boots for a moment before he thought better of it and sat across from Herb in an antique high-backed armchair that was too small for him.

"That's Susan's chair," said Herb.

"I know you're upset," said Lyle. "All I can say is that I'm sure they're safe. You shouldn't worry about them."

Herb looked out the front window and watched a young man in a t-shirt and cut-off jeans pushing a manual lawnmower across a lawn on the other side of the street. He saw Mr. Kwong next door holding his son's hand, the boy looking up at his father, as the two of them walked down the path toward their front door. When he looked back at Lyle he noticed dark blotches beneath the arms of his work shirt and patches of grease on his pant legs. Lyle looked back at him almost serenely, rasping slightly with each breath.

"Just tell me you know," said Herb. "Tell me you know where they are."

"What good would that do? What difference does it make if I know where they're gone?" Lyle sniffed and looked at the puddle drying on the carpet and the discarded shirt and his eyes followed the severed phone cord across the room to the dent in the wall.

"How long had she planned this?" said Herb.

"You need to straighten yourself out," said Lyle. "I think if you were capable you'd have done it by now. But you still need to try. Don't look for them. It'll make it worse. And it's best if you stay away from Joan. She won't talk to you." He stood to leave.

"If you need to talk to someone, you speak to me," said Lyle.

"I could use some cash," said Herb, standing, picking up the hammer by its head, tapping the shaft against his thigh.

"You still have a job, Herb. You're still an able-bodied man. Not some bum on the street." Lyle turned and went out the door and Herb followed.

"Just a loan," said Herb. "Until I get . . . organized." He gestured with the hammer as he spoke, standing in the doorway in his sleeveless undershirt, his pants sagging and his suspenders hanging down to his knees.

July, 1978

"Goodbye, Herb. Do whatever it is you need to do." Lyle opened the car door and got inside.

"Son of a bitch," shouted Herb. He walked onto the driveway. The engine turned over and an Eddie Arnold tune blared out of the open window as the Buick backed out. The car was pulling away when Herb let the hammer fly. He aimed low and threw without all his force, and the hammer struck the chrome of the rear bumper and fell harmlessly on the asphalt. The car slammed to a halt and Herb watched Lyle turn in his seat and look back at him, his impassive expression giving way to pity and disdain. Then he turned back around and the engine revved and the car accelerated down the street.

The young man with the lawn mower stood and watched as Herb walked out into the street in his sock feet. As soon as Herb picked up the hammer he returned to his work as if nothing out of the ordinary had happened. Herb walked back down the driveway and out of the corner of his eye he saw the Kwong boy staring at him from the front window. Strands of the boy's black hair stood straight up, clinging with static to the chiffon drapes that obscured the room behind him. Herb looked the boy in the eye and swung the side of the hammer's head into the palm of his left hand and went on into the house.

Herb righted the end table and put down the hammer. He picked up the phone and something rattled inside it and he tossed it back in the corner. In the bedroom he took a short-sleeved shirt from its hanger and put it on, buttoning the middle three buttons. He slid his suspenders over his shoulders and sat on the bed to put his shoes back on. He paused after tying the first lace, remembered lying there in that room, watching Sue as she extended her bare leg, sliding on her nylons, recalled the touch of her white linen uniform, the scent of baby powder and starch.

Then he picked up the phone on the night stand and dialled his mother's number.

"Hello?" she said. "Hello? Is that you, Herbert?"

His throat began to swell. He knew if he were to speak she would hear only the slurred despair of his father's voice, as if calling from beyond the grave. He hung up the phone and walked out of the room.

He went into the bathroom, urinated, and turned to face the mirror. He took off his horn-rimmed glasses and polished the lenses with the corner of his shirt. When he put them back on he saw patches of stubble on his broad cheeks. He recalled the searing morning headache, his unwillingness to turn on the bathroom light while he shaved. Then he noticed more tufts of white in his dark, crewcut hair than he had ever seen before. Opening the medicine cabinet he took a bottle of Listerine, gargled, and spat in the pink porcelain sink. Then he splashed cold water on himself and dried his face with a green towel hung on a hook on the back of the door.

He patted his right haunch and felt the slight bulge of his empty wallet. In the living room he sat down at the writing desk, took the scissors from the middle drawer and worked at the cardboard and the cellophane until all ten coins were loose. He stood, slid the coins into his right front pocket. Before he left, he looked over the living room and except for the dent in the wall and his dirty shirt and the stain on the floor the room looked to him as it did when he would come home late on Sue's nights off, after she had tidied up and the girls had gone to bed. He did not bother to lock the door after himself. Walking down the driveway he heard the sound of a dog barking, a radio playing. He smelled fresh cut grass and the odour of a charcoal barbeque. As he made his way down the street he looked back at the Kwong's but the window was empty and so was the driveway and there was no one there to see him leave.

Alice and Roy

June 19, 1981

Dear *Down Beat*,

I am writing out of dismay at Mr. Glasner's piece on Eleanora Sinclair in last month's issue. Glasner's assertion that the small acclaim enjoyed by Ms. Sinclair is due primarily to her strange disappearance only betrays his ignorance of vocal jazz and shows the same penchant for crude sensationalism exhibited by the mainstream media. The suggestion that she orchestrated her own disappearance as a publicity stunt is a joke of exceptionally poor taste—an insult to both Ms. Sinclair and her devout fans. Many of us consider her to be one of the greatest vocalists of her era. It is absurd to think that anyone who loved the stage as much as Ms. Sinclair would wilfully abandon public life. Dean Glasner should stick to writing about the bop and post-bop he gets off on, and leave Sinclair fans in peace.

        Alice Alderson
        New York, NY

* * *

In a Mist

July 7, 1981

Dear *Down Beat*,

I couldn't agree more with Alice Alderson's defence of Eleanora Sinclair. Too often, as in Mr. Glasner's piece, Ms. Sinclair is dismissed as a second rate performer. Indeed, the editors of *Down Beat* may be responsible in part for her status as a footnote in jazz history. Since Earl Ehrlich's short article following her disappearance in 1950, *Down Beat* has all but ignored her impressive catalogue and wide-ranging influence. Even Ehrlich's piece focusses on the circumstances of her disappearance and virtually ignores her merits as a distinctive, perhaps incomparable jazz vocalist.

I applaud Ms. Alderson for her criticism of Glasner, and would like to extend this criticism to the *Down Beat* establishment on the whole. Eleanora Sinclair ought to be remembered for her artistry, and not treated like pulp for the tabloids.

p.s. Any *Down Beat* readers who happen to live in the Fredericton/Oromocto NB area would be well-advised to tune into CHSR 97.9 FM every Thursday at 10 pm for *Two Drink Minimum*. Those of you who recognize that the show borrows its name from Sinclair's signature song (originally by Art Beazley, though Eleanora really made it her own) will require no further introduction.

> Roy MacArthur
> Fredericton, New Brunswick

* * *

Alice and Roy

July 26, 1981

Dear Roy,

We have finally had a chance to take a look at the piece you submitted back in February on Bix Beiderbecke and the Wolverines. Unfortunately, it's not the sort of thing we're looking for right now. F.Y.I., we don't as a rule consider unsolicited manuscripts.

Also, we won't be running your response to Ms. Alderson's letter. However, as a personal favour, from one Beiderbecke enthusiast to another, I can forward a copy of your letter to her, though I can't guarantee she'll respond. All the best with your radio show.

> Yours,
> Allan Brookes
> Asst. Editor, *Down Beat Magazine*

* * *

Five months after *Down Beat* publishes Alice Alderson's letter, Roy stands outside a gas station on the outskirts of Fredericton, duffel bag in one hand, a Greyhound bus ticket in the other. Roy is not about to let a conviction for dope deter him from attempting to cross the border. He's more or less kicked the habit and it seems unfair to him that such a trivial offence should keep him from accepting Alice's invitation. Roy's major concern right now is the handful of listeners who tune in regularly to *Two Drink Minimum* and the punker-angst rock they'll be subjected to during his absence. That week, between customers at the record store, Roy spent hours meticulously selecting tracks and scripting anecdotes for next Thursday's show. But in addition to covering his shifts while he was away, Roy's co-worker Andy agreed to sit in as the host of *Two Drink Minimum* only on the condition that he be permitted to play whatever records he wanted.

Three days later Roy is strolling down East Houston Street, arm in arm with Alice Alderson. He cleared the border without a hitch. Customs did not run a background check, nor did they detect the flask of rye in the inside pocket of his overcoat. Roy has forgotten what day of the week it is. He is not sure if he is in love, he only knows that he is profoundly elated to be in the company of the young woman at his side, and that he is overwhelmed. Roy is not used to big cities and he is not used to Alice. Their first few days together have been awkward at times, but they have also turned out better than Roy had expected. Though Alice proved to be the confident, opinionated young woman of her letters, Roy knows that in person he could never live up to the dashing persona of his radio broadcasts; which, at little prompting from Alice, he had tape-recorded and sent to her. Alice is not entirely disappointed with the young man she has met, but neither is she swept off her feet. Roy knows this. He also knows that his reticence is nothing a few pulls from his flask can't remedy. Alice likes it when he does this, not only because it helps him loosen up, but because it was a stylish thing for a young man to do.

Though Alice has had ample opportunity to become acquainted with Roy's voice, he is still growing accustomed to hers. They had spoken only once before meeting, and Alice had steadfastly refused to sing over the phone. When Roy requested that she send him a recording of herself, she complained that she had never had the opportunity to be professionally recorded—which is why, on the morning after Roy's arrival, as they sat drinking coffee in Alice's tiny apartment, there was an anxious smile on her lips as she

Alice and Roy

pushed the *Village Voice* across the table and pointed out the advertisement she had circled:

Jazz Vocalists Wanted. Silhouette Studios seeks undiscovered talent to audition/record. $20 fee payable at time of session. Serious inquiries only.

It is the afternoon of Alice's audition and they stand beneath an overcast sky in front of an East Houston Street newsstand. The proprietor is half a foot shorter than Roy and on his head is a grey watch cap. A cigarillo protrudes from his lips. His small, covered stand is stocked with the usual assortment of newspapers, magazines, candy bars and confections. It is only upon closer inspection that Roy notices many of the papers are yellowed around the edges, and some of the celebrities on the magazine covers have died. All the periodicals, in fact, are out of date. There are brittle copies of the *Times* from the late sixties, issues of *Esquire* and *Playboy* from the seventies.

"You brought a friend this time," says the man, nodding at Alice. He speaks with a slight accent that Roy cannot place. Alice reaches for something tucked behind a row of *National Geographics*, and when the May 1950 issue of *Down Beat* is revealed, he knows why she has brought him here.

The newsman takes the cigarillo from his lips. "This one is very rare, very hard to find." His brings his left hand to his mouth, covering his lips from Alice's view, as if to conspire with Roy. "For you, only twenty dollars," he whispers. "Make a nice gift for the lady."

Roy knows the man is asking far too much and he guesses that the man knows it too. While he imagines the LPs he could buy with twenty American dollars, he watches Alice flip through the pages. She stops at Ehlrich's feature, which is tastefully but predictably illustrated with the quintessential profile shot of Eleanora Sinclair in performance at Café Society circa 1948. Roy's romantic inclination is to agree with the man, to buy the magazine on the spot. The newsman winks at him. Roy reciprocates to appease him, but then checks his watch impatiently. Beneath them, the sidewalk rumbles and Alice looks up.

"The stop is right there," says the man. "You can make it if you run."

Alice returns the magazine, grabs Roy's hand and leads him in the direction of the subway.

"You're not going to buy it?" the man calls after them.

On the cramped train, pressed close to Roy, Alice speaks into his ear.

"The last time I looked at the magazine he told me I didn't need to pay in cash, that I could settle up another way."

By 98th Street their car is nearly empty. Roy looks over his shoulder and observes two women seated at the back. One is black, slim and poised. Her companion, by comparison, is pale and diminutive. Both wear stilettos, too much make-up and tight, revealing skirts. Roy nudges Alice and gestures with his eyes.

"Don't you have whores where you're from?" she asks.

"I suppose so," says Roy. "Not that I've ever had to pay for it." Alice pinches his arm.

At the next stop Roy follows Alice off the train and into the failing daylight. They walk north for several blocks and when Roy suggests they got off a stop too early, Alice responds that he gets to see more of the city this way. When they reach 138th Street they come to a diner with a painted sign that reads "The Bridgeview," and as Roy looks for the bridge, Alice opens the door and motions for him to follow.

Roy notices, as they seat themselves in a booth, that the women from the subway are sitting across the aisle.

"Don't you want to find the place first?"

Alice shakes her head. "It should just be another half a block down."

"Aren't you nervous? I can never eat when I'm nervous."

"Then just have coffee."

"I never said I was nervous. I just thought that you might be."

A young black waiter in a white t-shirt approaches and says, "Mm-hm?"

"Just a coffee."

"Grilled cheese and fries."

Roy turns up his nose. Alice swings her foot under the table and taps him on the shin.

When the waiter has come and gone again and his coffee cup is filled, Roy discreetly pours in whiskey from his flask. But he is not so discreet that Alice will not notice, and at the appearance of the flask, her foot touches his leg once more. Roy drinks and as he lowers the cup from his lips he is smiling until he looks around the restaurant and in the back corner sees what cannot be. Beyond the haze of the warmth in Roy's stomach and the grease in the air sits the Houston Street newsman. The newsman smokes a new cigarillo and has removed his watch cap to reveal his balding head. In front of him there is a steaming bowl and a cup like the one Roy holds in his hand. The newsman pays no attention to these things but looks intently across the room, his gaze fixed in the direction of the booth directly across from Roy and Alice. Roy averts his gaze and watches Alice toy with the packets of milk on his saucer. He leans in and whispers, "The man from the newsstand is sitting in the far corner."

"How is that possible?"

Roy shakes his head and looks again, not because he is unsure of what he has seen, but because he cannot help but look. When Alice goes to the restroom Roy turns in the direction the newsman is looking. The prostitutes sit smoking and laughing, watching the door to see who enters and who leaves. On the wall behind them hangs a photograph of someone who looks like Art Beazley. The black prostitute, Roy decides, is in fact a man. She is better dressed than her companion; from this distance, she is decidedly the more attractive of the two. The shorter woman—a girl, really—wears a white felt hat with a turned-down brim that might have been stylish once but has lost its shape, giving its owner a pitiable, juvenile look.

The waiter places Alice's sandwich on the table. "We're closing in fifteen minutes."

"Is that Art Beazley in that photo?" Roy asks.

"None other than." The waiter fills his cup without asking.

As Alice returns from the restroom, she scarcely looks at the man sitting in the corner.

"What do you think he's doing here?"

Alice shrugs her shoulders. "Having dinner."

"Has he seen us?"

"I don't think so. He's got other things on his mind." Alice nods in the direction of the prostitutes, and demurely swallows a mouthful of her sandwich.

Roy smiles and says, "I think the tall one's more your type."

Alice places her napkin on her plate and wraps her scarf around her face.

"You find it cold in here?" asks Roy.

"I'm going. I don't want to stay here any longer." Alice puts on her coat. "I'll meet you at my place afterwards. You can find your way back from here?"

Alice and Roy

"You sure you don't want me to come along? I'd like to see this studio."

"You'll just make me uncomfortable. I'll let you listen to the recording as soon as I get home. One of us has to stay and settle the tab."

Alice leaves and a moment later the prostitutes make their way to the cash. As the shorter woman asks the waiter for a pack of Pall Malls, the newsman approaches, puts his arm around her and tries to kiss her. When she protests he grabs her by the arm and with his other hand he produces his wallet and insists on paying for her. Roy cannot quite make out their conversation, but he sees the waiter point to the newsman, then to the door. The newsman swears and pounds the counter with his fist, and the few remaining customers begin to take notice. Before the waiter can get out from behind the counter, the transvestite steps in and removes the newsman's hand from the girl's arm.

As they walk out together the waiter blocks the newsman's path and says, "Best wait here until they're gone."

The newsman throws his hands in the air and at that moment from the dimness of the street there is a panicked scream, and then what Roy imagines must be the sound of a gun, and then silence. The newsman runs out the front door and Roy follows. Outside he sees the newsman kneeling beside the girl, who lies motionless on the sidewalk. There is a dark trickle running from her mouth to her chin. There are tears in the newsman's eyes and he does not notice Roy. There is no sign of the girl's companion and there is no sign of Alice. In the distance is the sound of sirens as Roy hurries down the street.

He is out of breath when he reaches the corner where the studio should be and is greeted by a graffiti-covered facade with plywood over its windows and a door that does not open.

Up the street, a bearded man with no laces in his boots has never heard of a place called Silhouette Studios, and is in need of thirty-five cents. Roy reaches into his pocket and hands the man a quarter.

He smiles. "Check the book in the phone booth around the corner."

Roy finds the booth, where all the directory pages between "Q" and "V" have been torn out. He picks up the phone, not knowing whom he intends to call. He reaches a hand into his empty pocket, then slams the phone into the receiver in frustration. From the top of the phone something falls to the ground that is immediately familiar to Roy, though in the twilight he does not recognize it to be Alice's address book until he holds it close to his face. It is open to the page for Silhouette Studios. Roy closes the book and attempts to place it in the inside pocket of his coat, which holds his half-empty flask. He shoves the bottom half of the book in his outer pocket as he makes his way back to 138th Street.

The girl's body no longer lies on the sidewalk. There is no ambulance, or police car, or any sign that anything at all has happened. Roy tries the door to the diner and finds it locked. Inside the waiter mops the floor. When Roy bangs on the window with his fist the waiter mutters something inaudible and points to the "Closed" sign on the door. Roy works his way down the street, trying every door along the way.

The fifth door is unlocked. Inside is a musty, narrow, high-ceilinged storeroom. Light from a single bare bulb illuminates a closed door at the end of the room. The walls are lined with metal shelves piled with old newspapers and magazines that spill out onto the floor. From behind the door at the back of the room there comes a sound and Roy decides he does not want to wait for the door to open. On his way out, he stumbles over a stack of *New Yorkers* and sends them scattering. Someone yells at him from behind.

Roy finds a train waiting at the bottom of the 135th St. stairs. He struggles through the turnstile and onto the nearest car without pausing to find out where the train is bound. Roy collapses in a seat and tries to still his shaking hands. Across the aisle, reading a copy of the *Amsterdam News*, sits the waiter from the restaurant.

"Excuse me."

The waiter looks up, sees Roy and turns back to his paper.

"Could you tell me where I could find Silhouette Studios?"

The waiter's expression softens. "You're on the wrong side of town. You want *West* 138th. Get off at the next stop, turn yourself around. You play?"

"No. Not really. My girlfriend sings."

"Does she now? That's alright." The man turns back to his paper, humming a tune that Roy does not recognize.

"Thank you," says Roy, as he gets off the train.

"Mm-hm," says the man.

Roy surveys the platform while he awaits the southbound train. The faces of those around him are turned away as he tips his flask to his lips.

An hour after he last sees Alice, Roy sits in the lobby of Silhouette Studios, his head in his hands. The radiator ticks with heat. There is an empty water cooler, a half-empty coffeepot, a table covered with scribbled sheet music, and the withered leaves of a dying aspidistra. There are framed forty-fives on the wall, and above a closed, padded door an illuminated sign that reads "Recording: Do Not Enter." Roy wants to examine the sheet music, to read the labels on the forty-fives, but his uneasy stomach and his throbbing head will not allow it. From the direction of the control room drifts the sounds of the session.

> *Oh , if you wouldn't mind,*
> *I'd find it divine,*
> *if I could tickle your funny bone.*
> *Some girls like to dance*
> *to be gently romanced,*
> *but I'd like to tickle your funny bone.*
> *No need to be shy,*
> *better to moan than to cry,*
> *oh so sweetly I'd tickle your funny bone.*
> *Twenty dollars no less,*
> *just a drop, not a mess,*
> *such a treat when I tickle your funny bone.*

The voice that sings is not Alice's and the song makes Roy want to leave. There is a piano break and the padded door opens to reveal a squat, rumpled man with horn-rimmed glasses and rolled-up sleeves. He raises his eyebrows and looks at Roy.

"I'm looking for Alice Alderson," says Roy.

"Alderson . . . Called to get directions, said she'd be late, never showed."

* * *

It is not until Roy returns to the empty apartment and checks the answering machine that he realizes her address book is no longer in his coat pocket.

"Listen," says the voice on the machine, "meet me back at the storeroom on 138th and I'll tell you where to find her. Don't tell no one where you're going and don't bring no one with you."

Roy barely makes it into the bathroom before he vomits.

He lies on the rumpled sheets of Alice's unmade bed. The apartment provides no comfort without her. It is as cold and indifferent to Roy's presence as the rest of the city. His head aches. He rolls over, opens the drawer of Alice's bedside table, and scrounges for a bottle. His hand falls on a photograph, and when he examines it in the dim light he sees Alice standing in a park in the summer heat, her arm around another woman he does not recognize. He swallows two tablets from the bottle, drinks as much water as he can keep down, puts on his coat, and is back on the street in minutes, on his way to the train.

The motion of the train makes his head spin and he is relieved to get off at 135th, though he does not look forward to what must follow. At the storeroom again, this time he knocks on the door, and the newsman, still smoking, greets him. As though in a gesture of good faith, he returns Alice's address book. He then hands him a small, limp package the size of a woman's purse, wrapped in newsprint and bound with string. "You need to make a delivery," the man says. "You deliver this for me."

Roy's head throbs, and it is hard for him to stand, though he doesn't dare to sit down. He wonders what might happen if he were to vomit on the magazines strewn about the floor.

"And then you will tell me where Alice is?"

The man smiles sadly, and nods, as if he would tell Roy then and there where Alice is, but he cannot because there is something Roy must do for him first.

"You deliver this to the river. Go down to the bridge and put this in the river, and I'll tell you where she is."

Roy wants to know why the man doesn't do it himself, how the man will know if Roy has done what has been asked of him, and the newsman says, "I'll know," without Roy having to ask.

Outside, away from the lingering scent of cigar, Roy makes his way toward the bridge, which the newsman has told him he will find at the end of 138th. It should make for a short, brisk walk, but there is fear and substances in Roy's blood that make the walk otherwise. To steel his resolve Roy imagines that he is of another era, a young hustler making a name for himself in the big city, all keyed up on dope with nothing to lose, running errands for some racket fronting as a late-night delicatessen. He walks past the Bridgeview, past the boarded-up facade on the corner, until in the distance he sees the darkness of the Harlem river.

It is then Roy happens upon the Wolverine Lounge. There is a brightly lit marquee and he can hear the sounds of swing coming from inside. It is precisely the sort of place he imagined he would find in New York and he thinks, if the night had turned out differently, he might have taken Alice here, told her the story of how a talented cornet player named Bix Beiderbecke found his way to New York fifty years before, only to drink himself to the grave at the age of twenty-eight. As he passes under the marquee, a man and a woman emerge from the club. The man is older than the woman, and dressed entirely in black.

"Roy!" says the woman, who after she smiles and speaks, is obviously Alice. "This is Roy," she says to the man, who also smiles, coyly, and extends his hand.

"You'll never guess who I happened to meet, Roy."

"Dean Glasner," says the man. "Pleased to make your acquaintance."

Roy's throat constricts as he shifts the weight of the parcel onto his left arm, and extends his right hand to meet the hand of Glasner. The parcel slips slightly. The old newsprint gives way and Alice screams as little moist red bits resembling teeth and severed fingertips clatter onto the sidewalk and come to rest in the flickering neon light of the Wolverine Lounge marquee.

Edgar and Morty

The gypsies packed up and left the grove just as the rain began to fall. That afternoon, after the storm broke, Edgar and Morty found plenty of dead-fall on the ground, scattered about the muddy ruts where the wheels of the caravans had rested. Edgar picked up a branch, grasped it with both hands and struck it against the trunk of an oak tree as if it were an axe.

"I'm glad that storm chased those nasty gypsies away. What are you up to Edgar?"

"I'm whacking fallen branches against trees. It's a game I've just invented."

"That's boring and dumb."

Despite Morty's show of disapproval, Edgar knew this was exactly the sort of pointless activity he enjoyed, and was not at all surprised when he claimed the largest branch as his own and reduced it to splinters against the trunk of an oak, making its branches sway and causing more leaves to fall. Morty was abnormally broad and hairy for a ten-year-old. He had appalling breath and a grotesquely mangled patch of skin on his right forearm, a scar he claimed to have acquired while helping his father butcher a leg of lamb. Morty never raised his voice above a hoarse whisper. He always sounded rather as though had been yelling severely the day before. Several of the older children in the village remembered a time when he could speak like anyone else, and it was rumoured his father had once forced him to drink boiling water. Whenever this was mentioned in Morty's presence, he would shove the offender into the mud and sit on his head. Other children tended to dislike Morty. They disliked him even more than they disliked Edgar. In fact, a good deal of dislike that would normally have been levelled at Edgar was diverted by Morty, and though he never said so Edgar was grateful for this.

"Edgar."

"What is it, Morty?"

"You're a bastard."

"Piss off Morty."

"Go knob your mother."

There was nothing Edgar could say at times like this other than "Piss off," for he really was an illegitimate child. Sometimes Morty would remember that Edgar's mother was dead, in which case he would say, "Go knob your dead slut mother." These perpetual insults were punctuated with an occasional shove in the mud, so Edgar would not forget that along with being an orphaned bastard, he was also small and weak.

The two boys had just about exhausted their supply of dead-fall when they came to the withered old oak at the edge of the grove. Edgar gave the tree a good whack and was winding up for a second when he noticed something protruding from a hollow at the base of its trunk. He dropped down, soiling the knees of his trousers as he stuck his head in the narrow opening. The darkness of the hollow, it seemed, was filled with crumpled newsprint. He had barely begun to investigate when he was interrupted by a tremendous pain in his rear-end.

"Piss off," he screamed, his voice muffled by the trunk of the oak.

"You deserve it," said Morty. "Why do you have your head in a tree like a bastard?"

The question, Edgar realized, was inevitable.

"Thought I saw something but turns out there's nothing in there," he said, having extracted himself, he hoped, in a casual enough manner.

"Let me have a look!" demanded Morty.

"Why? So I can wallop your rear-end? There's nothing in there, Morty."

"Out of the way!"

Morty shoved him aside with a good deal more force than necessary, and Edgar tottered and fell in a puddle, thoroughly soiling the clean parts of his trousers. Morty stuck his head in the tree as Edgar wiped the grime from himself.

"Liar," whispered Morty, withdrawing his head from the hollow. "You're a lying bastard. There's newspapers in there. You were reading papers like a bastard."

"That's right," said Edgar. "Why don't you tell me what I was reading about?"

"Reading's for bastards," said Morty. "I should wallop you for reading!"

"I'm going home now," said Edgar, his bottom still smarting. "It's getting dark. Besides, this tree-whacking game is dumb."

"I know," said Morty. "That's what I told you. See you tomorrow." Morty proceeded to lumber off in the direction of the butcher shop where he lived with his father.

Edgar made a show of strolling in the opposite direction, toward his grandmother's. As soon as Morty was out of sight, he crept back to the edge of the grove, glancing over his shoulder to ensure he was not being followed. The last traces of grey daylight slipped behind the hill as he approached the withered oak. He stuck his head inside the hollow once more, and drew aside the crumpled newsprint to reveal what lay beneath. In the dimness of the hollow he could discern the faintest metallic glint. He ran his fingers over the treasure he had found: four necklaces, two with jewelled pendants; three bangles; five rings; and handfuls of coins beneath it all. He thrust the coins in his pockets until they bulged to overflowing. He placed the necklaces around his neck, concealing them beneath his shirt and placed the bangles on his slender wrists. He held his arms out into the darkness before him and stumbled out of the grove. The pendants clinked softly together as he made his way along the path to the outskirts of the village. Clouds obscured the moon and the stars. The sky was black as pitch.

* * *

His grandmother let him keep a silver coin, claiming the rest of the loot as her own.

"Gypsy treasure is wicked," she warned, "and is not to be squandered by little boys."

Edgar protested the injustice, but in the end there was nothing he could do. Malevolent thoughts filled his head that night as he drifted off to sleep.

When he awoke the next morning the sky had cleared and the mud puddles had begun to to dry. He went into the village to console himself with the luxuries his single coin might afford. At the druggist's he purchased a pocket-sized edition of *Mutiny on the Sierra Madre*, and with his change he bought sweets, one for himself and one for Morty. He returned home and had read halfway through the second chapter when Morty banged on the door and demanded he come outside. Edgar discreetly tucked the novel beneath his shirt, unwilling to leave it behind.

Even after devouring the sweet Edgar gave him, Morty was in a particularly nasty mood, and though restless did not feel like doing anything at all. The two of them ended up at the edge of the grove, lying in the grass on the hill, watching smoke issue from the chimneys of the village. Edgar did his best to keep quiet and made no mention of the treasure. Morty took up his favourite topic of discussion, which consisted of naming all the children in the village and describing the terrible things he would like to do to them. This raised Morty's spirits somewhat, though Edgar had heard it all before and was bored. Morty soon became entirely engrossed in his morbid fantasies, gazing dreamily toward the pale blue sky. Unable to resist the opportunity, Edgar reached beneath his shirt and retrieved his book. He opened the paperbound cover and studied the ornate frontispiece, which featured a tri-masted galleon in flames and a sailor with two earrings and a cutlass between his teeth.

"Edgar," said Morty. "Do you think it would be worse to be put to death by the rack, or by flogging?"

Edgar looked up to find Morty glaring at him in a seething rage. Morty grabbed the book from his hands and was halfway down the hill before Edgar could protest. By the time Edgar caught up with him the book lay open face-down in a mud puddle, the heel of Morty's filthy boot applied squarely to its spine.

"Jesus bastard!" Edgar screamed, launching himself at Morty. He caught his adversary off-guard, having never dared attack him before. He landed on top of Morty with a muddy splash, but before Edgar could get to his feet, Morty was sitting on his head, demanding to know where the book had come from. Realizing the hopelessness of his predicament, Edgar spat out a mouthful of mud and proceeded to tell Morty about the treasure in the hollow of the withered oak, and how his grandmother had claimed it as her own, leaving him with a single coin.

"Selfish bastard!" Morty fumed, in his most terrifying whisper. "We could have shared the treasure and both been rich! I should kill you for lying." He contented himself with a brutal punch in the small of Edgar's back before lumbering off to the village.

* * *

Edgar and Morty hardly spoke a word to one another in the years that followed. Edgar's grandmother stashed the hoard in her own secret hiding place, and, on the first of each month, would present Edgar with a modest allowance he spent almost entirely on books. He often daydreamed of seizing the loaded pistol his grandmother kept beneath her bed, demanding to know the whereabouts of the treasure, running off with the riches to find a band of gypsies and appointing himself their leader. But he lacked the resolve of his favourite adventure heroes. His grandmother was in ill-health, and he decided instead to bide his time.

On his nineteenth birthday, with his grandmother on her deathbed, the whereabouts of the treasure were finally revealed to him. With her dying breaths, his grandmother told him she had been keeping the treasure safe until he became a man, so he would not squander his wealth. She instructed him to move to the capital and to use the money to pay for courses in the civil service.

Before the funeral Edgar visited his grandmother's hiding place in the attic and packed up the remaining loot. The supply of coins had been almost entirely depleted by this time. After the burial he travelled to the nearest town and sold the necklaces, bangles and rings to a jeweller, receiving a fraction of what he had once imagined they were worth. The money he returned with still made him one of the wealthiest men in the village.

It was around this time that Morty inherited the butcher shop from his father and Edgar decided he would no longer eat meat. From then on his sustenance consisted of bread, fish, fish soup, and the pots of ale he consumed every evening. Though he had long since given up on his dreams of gypsy life, he had neither the courage nor the desire to move to the city. Instead he decided that he would do absolutely nothing at all. With his fortune stashed in the bank, Edgar spent each night in the tavern and rarely woke before ten. In the morning he would read the newspaper before taking an afternoon stroll in the countryside, where he would pass without fail the grove on the hill where the withered oak stood. Returning to town, he would pay a visit to the baker and the fishmonger, and procure his daily provisions. Marguerite, the fisherman's daughter, who had once been an obnoxious and cheerful girl whom Morty spoke of disembowelling, had since blossomed into a busty and flirtatious young woman. She always made a point of letting Edgar know he was her best customer. Fresh fish in hand, Edgar would blush, return home, prepare his evening meal and make his way to the Black Boar where he would drink himself into a stupor.

He had been living in this manner for a little more than a year the day he encountered the falcon. It was an unseasonably warm afternoon and Edgar was laboured in his walking: the heat was oppressive, and a year of heavy drinking had taken its toll on his constitution. Doing his best to ignore the sweat on his neck, Edgar allowed his thoughts to wander. He recalled a story he had read that morning in the paper about a peculiar incident in a far-off country. A little girl from an orphanage had somehow gotten her hands on a pistol and had caused a scandal in church. During communion at Sunday mass she had produced the pistol from beneath her dress and taken a nun hostage, locking herself and her captive in the bell tower of the abbey. She promised to release the nun once she was shown proof of her mother's identity from the church records, given a sack containing the proceeds from the collection, and provided with a horse on which to make her getaway. The priest had apparently given in without much of a fight, not thinking the little orphan girl would get very far before she was apprehended. It was not until she had galloped off at tremendous speed that he was informed the girl was an experienced rider. As it turned out, the nuns who cared for the girl had permitted her to go for rides on Saturday afternoons, on a steed owned by a sympathetic farmer who had himself once been a young orphan with equestrian ambitions. Following the hold-up an effort was made to track down the girl's mother. But the woman had been of ill repute, and when she could not be found, the authorities assumed she had most likely come to an obscure and untimely end. No one had seen the girl since her escape and a sizeable reward had been offered for her capture.

Edgar was wondering what might have become of this orphan girl when he came across a rabbit nibbling clover at the edge of the grove. He was not of a disposition to have his emotions aroused by such sights, and paid the rabbit little heed. He spotted the falcon a moment later. It circled above at a great height before it swooped down to strike.

"Aiee!" exclaimed Edgar, covering his face with his arms. He watched from between his elbows as the stiffened rabbit was clutched up by the talons. The falcon circled once, answering Edgar's scream with a shrill cry of its own. Then, suddenly, it dropped the dead rabbit at Edgar's feet and flew off just as quickly as it had descended.

"Jesus," remarked Edgar, standing before the fresh prey. He had not seen a dead rabbit in years. His grandmother, from time to time, had bought them from the young men who would snare them and sell them at market. Edgar had hated to watch her skin their furry little carcasses, but he had always enjoyed a good bowl of rabbit stew. It then occurred to him how tired he was of fish. A bit of rabbit, he thought, might make for an agreeable change in menu. Edgar took the rabbit by its hind legs, slung it over his shoulder and continued on his way toward the village.

The bell on the butcher shop door jingled as he entered. Morty stood in the shadows at the back of the room, furiously cleaving the bloody flank of some huge beast. He did not look up from his work. After standing there for some time, holding the rabbit, Edgar cleared his throat. The butcher looked at him, finally, a glint in his eye as he wiped his blood-splattered hands on his soiled apron.

"I don't skin rabbits," he whispered, ending ten years of near silence between the two young men.

"My money's as good as anyone else's," said Edgar, laying his rabbit on the counter.

"Doesn't matter who you are," said Morty. "Don't skin rabbits as a rule." He smirked at Edgar. "No fish at the market today?"

"Today is an exception," Edgar replied. "Today I shall have rabbit for my dinner. I am prepared to pay twice what the job is worth. I will return to pick up my order before close."

He placed a coin on the counter and left it there. Morty said nothing, but looked at the rabbit with what Edgar chose to interpret as the irrepressible butcher's desire to rend flesh from hide. A silent agreement was then reached between the two men. Edgar bowed slightly to the butcher, and, like the falcon, left in the sudden and unexpected manner in which he had arrived. As he made his way out the door, Edgar thought he heard Morty whisper something, but he couldn't be sure.

Edgar was elated as he continued through the village. Instead of being angered by Morty's insolence, he was on the contrary pleased with himself for having taken the first step. It was with uncharacteristic joviality that he greeted the proprietor of the Black Boar. He brought a look of surprise to that man's moustachioed face when, instead of requesting his usual ale, he asked for wine. A bottle and a half later, Edgar left for Morty's shop with an exaggerated spring in his step. Edgar's usual reserve hijacked by the wine, he was seen executing a little twirl in the middle of the street by the boy who sold him his paper every morning.

"No fish today?" Marguerite called out from behind her cart, a smile on her lips.

"Not today," he replied. "Perhaps tomorrow."

He entered the butcher shop and made his way to the counter. It seemed somewhat farther from the door than he remembered.

"Thought you might have decided on fish after all," said Morty. He grinned, sliding a package on the counter, neatly wrapped in waxed paper and tied with string. The man's teeth really were awful, Edgar thought to himself, and the odour of his breath had certainly not improved, but rather, like a fine cheese, had grown more pungent and ripe with the passage of time. He suppressed a grimace, did his best to show his approval, and took the package under his arm. He was preparing himself to walk to the door in the semblance of a straight line when Morty placed a meaty hand on his left arm, extended the other hand, and pressed several small coins into Edgar's sweaty palm.

"No extra charge," said Morty. "But remember, from now on, no rabbits. You want real meat, you come to Morty the butcher."

"Of course," replied Edgar. "Many thanks." He turned and made his way to the door more hastily than necessary and felt relieved to be back out on the street, where the air did not smell of butcher's breath. All in all, he thought to himself, the exchange had gone rather well. Morty had been more amicable than he expected, offering him his change, treating him like any other customer. He did not think he had suspected him of drinking. And he wondered if perhaps Morty was no longer the raging imbecile he had once been. He would almost have been convinced had it not been for the unmistakable glint in his eye earlier that afternoon as he worked over the carcass at the back of the shop. This did not prevent Edgar from executing another little twirl before gingerly ascending the stairs to his apartment.

He poured a glass of wine and seated himself before his tidy package. The smell seemed a bit sour, he thought, as he untied the string. But it had been so long since he had dined on rabbit, he could not quite remember how it was supposed to smell. And besides, one had to admit, he was slightly drunk. His smile vanished the instant he found the bloody pelt. It was precisely the sight he had endeavoured to avoid. He could still make out the marks where the falcon's talons had gripped the creature. But these wounds seemed relatively humane compared to Morty's hack-job. He held his breath and inspected more closely, barely staving off the urge to vomit. Beneath the riven and bloodied pelt there was no meat: instead numerous beady unseeing fish eyes stared back at him from where the meat should have been. Edgar seethed, recalling Marguerite's mischievous smile as he passed by her cart that afternoon. He realized then that he had been the victim of a private little conspiracy between butcher and fishmonger.

"Bastards!" he cried. "Jesus bastards!" He took the wine bottle and held it to his lips, draining its contents in a single draught. Then he held the empty bottle by its neck and smashed it on the side of the table. Wielding the jagged edge of the bottle as if it were a dagger, he plunged it repeatedly into the fish-head-filled rabbit pelt until the package was reduced to little more than a puddle of blood, pulp, fish juice and fur. Then he began to blubber. He fell to the floor, moaning and sobbing with impotent rage. He felt utterly alone, loathing himself and his own stupidity as much as he loathed everyone he had ever known. He lay there for some time, until his sobs gave way to exhaustion.

Then, he began to feel a little better. Using the table to pull himself to his feet, he stood, wiped his fishy, bloodstained hands on his trousers, and wiped the wine and the tears from his face with his sleeve. As he regained his composure, the necessary course of action became entirely clear to him. He retrieved that morning's newspaper and tore out the article about the orphan girl and placed it beneath the pillow of his bed and used the rest of the paper to wrap up the mess on the table. Taking the pistol from beneath the bed seemed perfectly natural, as natural as taking up his walking stick for an afternoon stroll. He put on his coat and tucked the bundle of newsprint under his arm, as if taking along a bit of lunch for the trip. Blood started to show through the paper and he wrapped up a few more sheets before leaving.

It was rather late by the time he returned to Morty's shop, and the street was entirely deserted. Using the butt of the pistol, he smashed the lock on the door with ease, as if he were hammering a nail to hang a painting on the wall. Reality remained conveniently at bay until Edgar burst into Morty's upstairs apartment, only to discover the butcher naked on the floor, thrusting himself into Marguerite, equally naked, moaning blithely beneath him. Morty was as repulsive as his lover was fair, his broad, stumpy body completely covered in dark hair, save for the hideously scarred patch, still prominent on his right forearm. At the sound of the door the two of them turned to look at him, wide-eyed and panting. Edgar momentarily lost his nerve and almost turned to flee before it occurred to him that this particular turn of events would only simplify things. The two of them, the butcher and his buxom accomplice, could eat the rabbit-pelt-fish-head-puree together. If a little orphan girl could, by the barrel of a pistol, have her way with an entire abbey, then so could he serve justice to Morty the butcher and his fish-wench trollop. Rather unfortunate, he thought to himself, that he should only come to witness the full extent of Marguerite's endowments under present circumstances. Nevertheless, it was to his advantage in the business at hand that she should be caught and exposed in such a state.

Before him on the floor, supporting himself on his elbows, his manhood half engorged between his hairy legs, Morty spat at Edgar. The spittle landed between Edgar's feet, causing him to look down and notice, for the first time, the smudge of rabbit's blood on his boot. He raised the pistol and took aim, as if to erase the smug expression from the butcher's face by waving its muzzle. Marguerite gasped, cowering in the corner, covering her pale flesh with a sheet from Morty's unmade bed. Edgar was pleased with her reaction, and was about to remove his finger from the immediate vicinity of the trigger when Morty snarled, "Lose your appetite?"

"Bastard!" Edgar screamed. It was, he realized, the only coherent expression he had been capable of uttering since his nasty surprise. He retrieved a woman's shoe from the pile of petticoats and butcher's garments scattered about the floor. With an accuracy he could never have duplicated while sober, he threw the shoe at Morty, striking him under his left eye.

"For that you'll pay dearly!" threatened Morty.

"Perhaps!" cried Edgar, caught up in the moment, "But first, you shall dine. I may have lost my appetite, but surely you two have been busy working up healthy appetites of your own!" The table in the corner had already been set with bread, wine, and what looked suspiciously like fresh rabbit meat. Edgar gestured with the pistol.

"Hurry! Get dressed! Casually of course, for tonight is an impromptu affair." Edgar grinned with malevolence, delighted by his own cleverness. Morty struggled into his underpants as Marguerite fashioned a toga out of the bed sheet. Then they sat themselves at the table as Edgar had instructed. Marguerite filled two plates with the mess from Edgar's dripping parcel and Morty poured the wine. Edgar proposed a toast.

"To friendship! To the mutual beneficiaries of a thriving village economy!"

Morty and Marguerite had drained their glasses and were working up the resolve required to chew and swallow their first bite of fishy rabbit pelt when Marguerite began to cry. Though she enjoyed a practical joke now and then, she attempted to explain to Edgar through her sobs, she had meant no harm and thought their treatment at his hands altogether beastly and undue. Though not unmoved by her address, Edgar was dead-set in his intentions, and was about to threaten her beautiful bosom with his pistol, when, suddenly, Morty himself burst into tears.

"I am sorry," he proclaimed, in his parched whisper. "After all these years, it was a nasty thing to do. But I beg of you, do not go through with this. Free meat for a full year if you surrender your pistol! Cuts of the finest quality. With Marguerite as my witness!"

Edgar had never seen Morty so repentant, so vulnerable. He wondered what the little orphan girl would do if she were to find herself in this situation. It occurred to Edgar he was not cut out to be a successful outlaw. Half moved to pity by Morty's plea, and, it must be admitted, half wanting to inflict further humiliation upon the grovelling butcher, Edgar said the first thing that came into his head.

"Look at you, Morty. Your father ruined you." Perhaps Morty knew this to be true, perhaps he hated Edgar all the more for saying so.

"And that wretched gypsy fortune ruined you," declared Morty, with all the conviction his whisper would allow.

Still half expecting Morty to ram him headfirst into the wall and pound him to a pulp, Edgar lowered the pistol. Marguerite slumped in her chair and uttered a sigh of relief. Morty pushed himself back from the table, retrieved a third glass from the cupboard, filled it with wine and handed it to Edgar. Edgar gratefully accepted, seating himself on the edge of Morty's bed.

"I suppose that was what you were thinking when I came to pick up my rabbit this afternoon."

Morty nodded.

"You could barely walk."

Edgar winced, not prepared to let the conversation dwell for too long on his own vices.

"It was not pleasant to have no parents of my own, but it must have been worse, I suppose, to have an ogre as a father."

"I wanted to kill him," confided Morty.

"That's so sad," said Marguerite, the bed sheet slipping slightly from her bosom.

The Death of Benjamin Hirsch

In retrospect, the signs of his passing were apparent days before I learned of the accident. It happened over the holiday, and at the time I thought nothing of the uncollected newspapers piled outside my upstairs neigbour's door, or the absence on the street of his Japanese sport coupe, with its tinted windows and excessive stereo system. For several days, no muffled footsteps, no dance music, no sound of men's laughter, nor fainter sounds of passion. I assumed he was out of town, visiting his relatives in New York, the peace and quiet an unintended Christmas gift to the man who lived below.

I did not find out the truth about Benjamin Hirsch until New Year's Eve. Holding a bottle of pinot noir and a box of Aquarius cigars, I encountered Leventhal in the front porch as he unlocked the door that leads to the upstairs flat. I might have assumed that Benjamin, who had always gotten along with the landlord better than I, had asked him to stop by and water the plants or to run the water so the pipes wouldn't freeze. I might have assumed this except for two details that were impossible for me to ignore. Leventhal, who had never been a particularly cheery man, appeared unusually solemn, this in spite of the fact that he was accompanied by the most beautiful woman I had ever seen.

In a Mist

"Benjamin out of town?" I asked.

The dark haired young woman, whom I was certain I had never met before, looked more than vaguely familiar. She wore a black wrap-over coat with a silver floral brooch, a brimless black cloche hat covering all but the tips of her curls. With her heart-shaped face and Cupid's- bow mouth, she struck me as the image of young Norma Talmadge, resurrected from the silver screen. My scrutiny must have been indiscreet, for she quickly averted her radiant eyes.

Leventhal stooped to collect the newspapers at his feet, a mixture of scorn and pity on his sagging features. He examined their headlines through his thick glasses, thumbing through them one by one. When he came across the date he wanted he presented it to me. Silently, the young woman made her way up the stairs. Now holding a copy of the *Sun Times*, in addition to the cigars and the wine, I watched her slender, black-stockinged ankles and her low-heeled pumps as they slowly ascended and disappeared from view. Before I could determine what was expected of me, I was handed a second newspaper. Leventhal's expression softened as he met my gaze once more. He sighed, briefly laying his right hand upon my shoulder before he followed the young woman up the stairs.

Once inside I placed the cigars and the wine on the table by the front window and sat down without bothering to remove my hat and coat. I began with the first paper, dated "December 30." On a hunch I started with the obituaries. I scanned the narrow columns until I came across what Leventhal had intended me to find.

Benjamin Hirsch, born April 9th 1976, died tragically on December 26th. He will be missed by his younger sister Lillian, family, friends and colleagues at Thornburg and Associates. Memorial service and interment to be held on Jan. 2nd, 2pm at Sunset Memorial Lawns, Northbrook Illinois.

The Death of Benjamin Hirsch

I then scanned the first section of the second paper, dated "December 27." The initial report was located halfway down the sixth page.

A twenty-eight year-old-man died of internal injuries when struck by a car at approximately 3 am on Thursday morning. The man, whose identity has not yet been released, was struck from behind while walking along West Webster Ave. just south of Halsted St. The driver fled the scene and remains at large. Poor visibility may have contributed to the accident though alcohol is suspected of having been a factor. Police are asking anyone who may have witnessed the accident to come forward.

The last time I spoke to Benjamin Hirsch was the night of December 23rd. He was bare-chested and unshaven when he answered the door. I could hear his companions in the background, their voices barely discernible over the music. Before I could bring the volume to his attention he smiled, apologized and promised to turn it down. I knew he would do so. He always did. I also knew that the sounds of their revelry, however hushed, would inevitably be heard long into the night. When I returned to my room I put on a Palestrina motet, adjusted the volume so that it was scarcely audible, and prepared to make the best of it. The next morning, in my robe and slippers, seated with tea and toast by the front window, I watched Benjamin walk out alone. In his fitted wool overcoat and sunglasses, he walked to his car, got in and drove away. I often wondered if he removed his sunglasses once behind the tinted windows.

My thoughts were interrupted by the sound of descending footsteps and the closing of the front door. From my window, through the growing darkness, I could make out the hunched, maundering form of Leventhal as he made his way down the empty street. Beside him, the elegant figure of Lillian Hirsch. Brotherless. Bereaved.

* * *

In a Mist

The "For Rent" sign appeared on the last Sunday in January. I called Leventhal as soon as it was posted and, after some negotiation, arrangements were made for me to move upstairs the following Monday. My rent would increase significantly. In fact, I would barely be able to afford it. Nevertheless, sometime in the dull hung-over hours of New Year's Day, I had resolved that a change was entirely necessary.

At the time, I was not optimistic about finding more lucrative employment. With two years of music history and film studies at DePaul University and a semester's experience at the campus bar, I had become resigned to the profession I had fallen into. I was not particularly attached to my job, but I found tending bar at the Tiger Rag preferable to the prospect of looking for work elsewhere. I got along alright with Jerome, an aspiring trumpet player from Washington Park, who worked the tables. And I respected the owner, Eddie O'Connell, a Canadian from Winnipeg, Manitoba. In middle-age, after an ugly divorce, estranged from his ex-wife and only son, Eddie had moved south to a town full of jazz clubs and managed to open a successful one of his own. Eddie prided himself on a peculiar notion of authenticity. Short of distilling the gin in a basement bathtub, he did everything he could to make the Tiger Rag the kind of prohibition-era speakeasy he was not quite old enough ever to have been inside. He would remark from time to time that running an over-the-table establishment took half the fun out of it. Jerome and I suspected he secretly funnelled half the profits from the bar to the temperance revival movement in the hopes that prohibition might one day be reinstated.

During my interview he asked me to make him an old fashioned. As I measured the rye whisky into a glass, he went over to an old upright Steinberg in the corner and plunked out a meandering melody. He stopped after a few bars and when I looked up he stared at me expectantly, eyebrows raised, fingers poised on the ivories.

"*In a Mist*," I said. "Beiderbecke's tune. The cornet player." He grinned at me and I knew I had the job. He liked that I was from Iowa, that I had grown up with the sounds of well-worn forty-fives, dragged to Dixieland festivals from the time I could walk, regaled with tales of paddle boat bands and pleasure house parlours. Though I knew enough about early jazz to engage Eddie in conversation, I did not share his enthusiasm.

"Us outliers must stick together if we're going to weather this city of the big shoulders." It occurred to me, even as he offered me the job, that there must be hundreds of people out of work and from out of state much more qualified than me to tend bar in an upscale establishment like Eddie's. We shook hands nevertheless. I agreed to show up at four the following afternoon so he could show me how to mix a more palatable old fashioned. Then he asked me if I liked men.

When he saw my reaction he tried to smooth it over.

"You've got the job one way or the other. I shouldn't have asked. I just like to know who I've got working for me is all. I'm sure you can appreciate that."

I did my best to assure him I had no interest in men. He smiled, nodded, apologized again for asking. Two years later, he still declined, when in my presence, to make the comments concerning the more attractive female customers he would freely exchange with Jerome.

The night after I arranged to move into the empty upstairs apartment was the night I saw her at the bar. It was a Monday, an unusually slow night at the Tiger Rag and, though I had only glimpsed her face for a moment on that afternoon following Benjamin's death, I was certain it was her, alone in the corner booth. She took off her coat and hat to reveal her long, loose, sleeveless dress and dark, close-cropped curls. She sat with her legs crossed and watched as Eddie sat down at the piano and began to play the "Wolverine Blues." Jerome approached her and she took a pen from her clutch and wrote on a napkin and he brought the soda water she requested. She lit a cigarette, only to extinguish it prematurely and light another a moment later. She produced a powder compact, examined herself in the mirror, and returned it to her clutch. It was as if she were waiting for someone. It occurred to me that she was waiting for Benjamin. I knew this was impossible, but nevertheless the scenario played out in my mind. The anticipation of the meeting, her early arrival, the ordering of the soda water so as to retain clarity of perception for the precise moment he appeared. That gradual, almost imperceptible transition from anticipation to anxiety as time passed and she remained alone. And then the threshold, the moment at which she loses hope, a phone call considered but not placed, anxiety given way to vexation. I wanted to go to her, to look her in the eye and tell her that he would not be coming, that she would never see him again. But I remained behind the bar and it was Jerome who collected her empty glass and that was when she ordered the dry manhattan.

The dry manhattan was a house specialty, the preparation of which, under Eddie's supervision, I had long since perfected. This time, however, at the last moment—after the Maraschino cherry was submerged, and without knowing precisely why I felt inclined to do so—I added a disproportionate quantity of sweet vermouth. I immediately regretted this decision. But there was no opportunity to start over, for Jerome hastened the drink to the occupant of the corner booth. I did my best not to look in her direction, and made some show of busily polishing wine glasses. And yet, without looking directly at her, in the periphery of my vision I discerned an unmistakable expression of disgust on Lillian's face as she put the glass down. This was followed, inexplicably, by a smile.

Though I had never been overly fond of her brother, with his trappings of professional and material and amorous success, his self-satisfaction, I was strangely upset by this peculiar smile on his sister's lips only four weeks after his death. I now looked openly across the room as she raised the martini glass to her lips and drained its sickly contents in a single, saccharine draught. A table of bourbon-swilling regulars arrived at that point, momentarily requiring my attention. Only a minute or two had passed, however, before Jerome requested another dry manhattan for the corner booth. This I prepared with but a modicum of sweet vermouth. I then emerged from behind the bar, approached Eddie at the piano and requested the rest of the night off on account of a sudden, incapacitating bout of nausea. Eddie agreed, on the condition I arrive early the following afternoon as he had something important to discuss with me before I started my shift. Outside, I hailed a cab instead of walking the three and a half blocks to where my car was parked.

* * *

As I lay in bed that night it occurred to me she might have left something behind, forgotten her hat, left a note at the bar in case her companion arrived after she had gone. But the following afternoon nothing remained to indicate her presence the night before save a single lipstick-stained cigarette, half-smoked, in the ashtray on the table in the corner.

Eddie was leaning back in his chair when I poked my head in his office. The surface of his desk was covered in empty low-ball glasses, coffee cups, accounting ledgers, back issues of *Down Beat* and the *Tribune*. He gestured to the empty chair, broke the news that he was opening a second club across town on the south side, to be called the Lotus Blossom. He then offered me the position of assistant manager of the Tiger Rag. There would be a considerable raise, effective immediately, though I would have to continue my duties as bartender until he hired a suitable replacement.

"When I make up my mind as to someone's character," said Eddie, "there's no two ways about it. My ex for example. I knew she was no good the moment I laid eyes on her." He grinned at me, and winked.

"Things happen for a reason. Even terrible things. Without the atrocities of the Civil War, how many cornet horns and marching snares would have found their way into French Quarter hawk shops?" It was a question I had never bothered to consider.

"If you hadn't dropped out of college after your grandfather died, who would I have to help me out? A man's got to take stock of who he is and what he really wants."

I accepted his offer without further hesitation. We shook on it. Eddie poured me a drink, and then another, and I went to work that afternoon, elated, in a soft scotch haze. That week, as I put in long hours learning the basics of managing the business by day, tending bar by night, Benjamin's worldly possessions were sold off, donated, cast out on the curb. I do not know if Lillian Hirsch paid another visit to her brother's apartment. During this time my only encounter in the front porch involved the two cleaning ladies Leventhal had hired the weekend before I moved in. Middle-aged Inez, and Maria, much younger, who took charge of introductions. On the day I took possession, I discovered that they had done a remarkable job of effacing virtually every trace of

Benjamin's existence from the upstairs flat.

Leventhal was unusually friendly when he presented me with the keys. He told me of his plans to renovate the downstairs apartment and increase the rent.

"You're doing me a favour. I was wrong about you," he called out, as he made his way down the stairs. "Thought I had you figured out but I was wrong."

Shortly after Leventhal left I happened upon the first in the series of objects that had, for whatever reason, survived the purge. On the floor in the back corner of the bedroom closet, I discovered a black velvet barrette, rhinestone studded, a single strand of dark hair curled in its silver clasp. The following afternoon, I came across a gold-labelled one-litre bottle of balsamic vinegar, one third full, in the cupboard beneath the kitchen sink. I poured the vinegar down the drain, rinsed the bottle and set it in the light of the sun on the sill of the kitchen window overlooking the street below.

It was not until almost a month later, when I gave the bathroom its first thorough cleaning since Maria and Inez had scoured it immaculate, that I made the third discovery. Though it was perhaps the most insignificant of the three, in my mind it forever has greater magnitude in that it was immediately preceded by an altogether different discovery, one entirely unrelated to my inheritance of wayward household objects. It was an unseasonably warm mid-winter day, February sunlight streaming down from the domed skylight overhead. By leaning my stereo speakers against the hallway wall at an angle of forty-five degrees so that they faced toward the bathroom ceiling, I discovered a peculiar quirk of the apartment's architecture. The sounds of Tallis's *Spem in Alium* reverberated with cathedral-esque resonance. The result was overwhelming. I stopped scrubbing and remained on all fours, eyes closed, like a supplicating monk, amidst the stringent aromas of lemon and pine and the faintest trace of stale urine, in a state of transcendence. I did not open my eyes again until the forty-voice motet reached its exultant conclusion. Still marvelling at my revelation, I finished cleaning the bathroom as I listened to Tallis's minor works. It was then I came across the condom. It was still in its package, lubricated, computer tested, hermetically sealed.

I thought then about Benjamin Hirsch. I knew so little about him. I wondered if he had been aware of the acoustic properties of his bathroom, if he would have appreciated the profundity of my revelation. What had his life been like before he had moved in? What effect had the apartment upon him, with its pristine hardwood floors and twelve foot ceilings, its miraculously powerful water pressure, its opulent fixtures? I thought of Lillian Hirsch, of my encounter with her at the bar, of the strangeness of my reaction. I thought about my grandfather, dead at sixty-seven, of the trip home to the funeral in Davenport and how I didn't return until four months later. I thought about Eddie, his ability to overcome loss, his courage in starting over, how this courage had paid off and how his subsequent good fortune had contributed to mine. I considered my promotion, how the move upstairs was not, as it might have been, a strain on my bartender's wages, but entirely appropriate given my new position as assistant manager of the Tiger Rag.

I realized, of course, that things could have just as easily gone the other way. Eddie had warned me from the outset that there was no guarantee his latest venture would prove successful, that my promotion might only be temporary. But the Lotus Blossom was thriving, and I was turning out to be a decent manager, somehow living up to Eddie's expectations. Sometimes I tried to make sense of the circumstances of Benjamin's death. I wondered what brought him to walk alone on West Webster Avenue in the early hours of December 26th. If disaster could strike down Benjamin, so young, so self-assured, why not me? And yet I could not help but feel that this fear was unfounded, that I had somehow become immune to misfortune. I was still alive, happily so, and would be, I was certain, for some time to come.

* * *

The day Benjamin would have turned twenty-nine happened to fall on Good Friday. After closing up the bar the night before, Jerome and I celebrated the long weekend and I overslept the following morning. It was early afternoon by the time I made it to Sunset Memorial Lawns. Benjamin's headstone was an obelisk, upright, tapering as it rose, greyer than the sky. No one was there when I arrived. I did not hear her approach from behind, though I felt her presence, just as I had felt the absence of her brother several months before. When I turned to face her I saw that her eyes were reddened, her features wan. Without her make-up she more closely resembled him. She wore her cloche hat, the same black wrap-over coat, now torn at the right cuff. In her arms she held a bouquet of lilies, their stems wrapped in silver cellophane. I did not know what to say to her. After her gaze passed through mine I knew it did not matter. She knelt and placed the flowers on his grave.

I turned to her once more. On this second glance the vacuity of her gaze was replaced by a tentative recognition. It was then I smelled the liquor on her breath. It occurred to me my association with her brother in her mind might serve my own end, that I might use this unlikely semblance, the feeling of knowing someone intimately—a stranger. The true nature of my relation to Benjamin was immaterial.

In a Mist

All that mattered was that I was there, at his grave, to console her for her loss. She did not recoil at my touch. Her face turned against my left shoulder, her hands upon the small of my back, I could feel her inaudible sobs. She was surprisingly receptive to my consolation. Or perhaps, given the circumstances—my proximity, our privacy, the profundity of her sadness—it was not surprising at all. Eventually she pulled away and stood by my side, staring at her brother's headstone. We remained there for some time, unspeaking, and then she walked away.

I almost called out to her. As I remember that moment I call out to her. I offer her a lift. She accompanies me to the Tiger Rag where I turn on the lights, make her a cup of coffee. Quietly, soberly, in the corner booth, I give my account of her brother. Somehow, with utter naturalness, as if the gradual, retroactive acknowledgement of something known all along, the truth comes out, dissonance giving way to harmonic resolution. This confession is not at all awkward, and requires little explanation. But I do not call out. Instead I stoop to collect the bouquet at my feet, and breathe the heady fragrance of the soft white trumpet bells.

The White Knight

The game of chess is a supernova, which can warm the backside of an amoeba, or incinerate an entire civilization.
                Pavel Rublev
                System Chess Champion, 2087-2091

My name is Frank Rinehardt and I am twenty-seven years old. I like racquetball, film history, hard liquor and chess. Up until a month ago I was a PhD candidate at Berkeley. My unfinished dissertation was on the use of chess as a metaphor in the films of Humphrey Bogart. There are those in the twenty-second century who believe Bogart was the greatest screen actor of his era. There is a smaller group that consider him to be one of the greatest artists of any era. Several key proponents of this dogma belong to the Film History Department at Berkeley. This was the dogma to which I subscribed, until recently.

On the evening of February 17th I poured myself a highball and went to bed after marking an entire seminar's worth of undergraduate assignments. In addition to my research, I was a teaching assistant for a third-year course on representations of the Second World War in twentieth century film. I had been asked to prepare a lecture on *Casablanca* and give the class an assignment based on my research. This was an entirely reasonable request, as the film comprised the longest chapter of my dissertation. I first saw the film by accident, as a bored undergraduate on a blind date, having met up with the wrong "red-haired Cynthia" in the lobby of the Brattle, a run-down 2-D repertory movie house. I had made plans with the other Cynthia to see Bergman's *The Seventh Seal*, but it was Valentine's Day and I had nowhere else to go and when the young woman in the lobby insisted on seeing *Casablanca*, I didn't make a fuss. She thought the film was trite. I disagreed. It wasn't until the next morning that she discovered I was the wrong Frank. But by that point it didn't matter. Despite our disparate tastes in twentieth-century cinema we've remained lovers ever since. And it was *Casablanca* that led to my interest in film history, and eventually to my specialization in chess metaphor scholarship. As I researched the film I discovered that the circumstances of its creation amounted to a series of peculiar accidents. In this respect the film seemed not unlike my own life. The only difference was that *Casablanca* was a masterpiece.

It occurred to me that if I could make sense of the film in a way in which no one had managed to do before, I might imbue my own life with a sense of purpose it seemed to lack. Through my graduate research, I became increasingly convinced that the magnificence of the film had nothing to do with the numerous writers who contributed to the final script, or the often chaotic circumstances of wartime film production, or Ingrid Bergman's initial failure to be cast as Maria in *For Whom the Bell Tolls*, or even the inspired direction of the churlish Michael Curtiz. It was my conviction that the most significant achievement in cinematic history must be credited entirely to Humphrey Bogart. Furthermore, this achievement had nothing to do with his acting ability, but was in fact a product of his life-long interest in chess.

The White Knight

As I explained to my students, the use of chess as a metaphor in *Casablanca* is extremely subtle. The entire film contains only a single chess scene, the chess board purportedly included by Curtiz only at Bogart's urging. The board appears at the moment we first meet Rick Blaine, the character that solidified Bogart's reputation as one of the greatest icons in the history of the silver screen. At 9 minutes, 14 seconds Rick is seated in his café, contemplating a chess game set up on a board before him. Ugarte, portrayed by Peter Lorre, is seated to his side. As Rick cautiously advances the White queen's knight to the fifth rank, Ugarte persuades him to hold some documents on his behalf. The documents in question are blank transit letters allegedly signed by General Charles de Gaulle, guaranteeing passage from Casablanca to the freedom of Lisbon. They will become the focus of the film, what Hitchcock would refer to as the *McGuffin*, or Lacan the *objet petit* a. At 11 minutes, 38 seconds, as Rick reaches for the letters, he accidentally knocks over the Black king directly in front of him. This is the instant upon which, traditionally, most *Casablanca* chess metaphor scholarship has centred. But if you ask me, and will excuse my metaphor, the Black king is in fact a red herring. The real crux of the scene occurs at 12 minutes, 5 seconds. This is when the White knight inexplicably vanishes from the board.

In order to understand the significance of the missing knight, one must first know something of Bogart's relationship with chess. He was a lifelong enthusiast of the game, a strong amateur player who achieved expert status according to 1950s US Chess Federation standards. His ability was perhaps best illustrated by his draw with Sammy Reshevsky in a 1955 simultaneous exhibition in Hollywood. Before he made a name for himself with *Petrified Forest*, Bogart would hustle at chess for dimes in

In a Mist

Times Square and Coney Island. After his acting career took off he continued to play both on and off the set. It is speculated that the solitary game in *Casablanca* was actually based on a correspondence match Bogart was playing at the time. His opponent remains unknown. What is known is that in 1943 the FBI paid Bogart a visit and insisted he cease his correspondence with European rivals. The FBI had been monitoring Bogart's mail and were convinced his chess notation contained encrypted information. In 1945, Bogart appeared with Lauren Bacall on the cover of *Chess Review*. During his interview he said he liked chess better than poker because you couldn't cheat at chess. Someone should have told that to the FBI.

The shot in question is the last involving the chess board in *Casablanca*. The camera is repositioned as Ugarte rises to collect a drink from the waiter, and the White knight, which has remained at the fifth rank since 9 minutes, 14 seconds, suddenly fails to appear on the board. Neither has Rick captured the knight and placed it to the right of the board in the company of the captured pawns. The knight is simply not there.

If this disappearance is acknowledged at all, it is dismissed as an oversight, a minor instance among several greater instances of discontinuity in the film. Inaccurate representations of chess are hardly unusual in twentieth-century cinema. Perhaps the most notorious example is the game astronaut Frank Poole plays against the computer HAL in Stanley Kubrick's *2001: A Space Odyssey*. The game was based on a real match that took place in Hamburg in 1910 between Roesch and Schlage. HAL declares Black's sixteenth move as "queen to bishop three," when in fact it is "queen to bishop six," and as a result Poole resigns unnecessarily. HAL's move is often cited as an error in the film, but Kubrick, like Bogart, was a strong chess player and it is much more likely the mistake is an early indication that something has gone terribly wrong with HAL's operating system.

Similarly, I contend that the missing knight in *Casablanca* is not an error at all. The knight's disappearance is the only anomaly of its kind I have been able to detect in Bogart's entire body of work. This is why it is so peculiar. How could such a careless oversight occur on a chessboard directly in front of a man with such an affinity for the game? Any self-respecting chess metaphor scholar who gives this instance due consideration must conclude that the disappearance is in fact deliberate, and the question must be rephrased: *Why did Bogart allow the disappearance to occur?*

This is the problem I posed to the students of the World War II film seminar. I asked them to discuss the significance of the disappearance in five hundred words and send in their response by Monday morning. As I explained the assignment the blank looks on their faces concerned me. On Monday morning their responses confirmed that the nuances of chess metaphor theory were beyond them. Though the brighter students knew their Bogart, they knew as little about chess as their peers. The game has fallen out of fashion. I doubted that any of the students had ever played, or even observed a game. Two or three made an effort to look up the rules and wrap their heads around the basics. One young woman even went so far as to cite classic opening gambits and comment on how the *Casablanca* opening appears to be a unique innovation on the part of Bogart's mysterious opponent. But alas, a rigorously applied understanding of the complexities of the game to the semiotic conundrum I proposed was simply too much to ask for in a five hundred word assignment. Most of the students did not even address the question at all. They simply regurgitated Bogart theory, some more eloquently than others, all of them no doubt finishing in time to make the latest zero-gravity orgy organized by the film history undergrad society.

As I lay awake in bed on the evening of February 17th, 2105, I thought about what my students had not bothered to consider. I contemplated the uniqueness of the knight. Unlike any other piece on the board, the knight does not move in a linear fashion, but in an 'L' configuration. It is also the only piece with the freedom to pass over chessmen in its path. Its movement is limited only by the outer boundaries of the board. The sudden foray of a knight can take even a highly experienced, calculating player by surprise. By passing through a solid object directly in its path, the knight achieves the sort of transportation particle physicists have only begun to understand in the last few years, and it has done so since fourteenth century Persia. If there is significance in the vanishing of the White knight, and I am convinced there is, then there is significance in its knighthood. It is as if the knight in *Casablanca* was shot mid-move, in the miraculous act of its transport from one square of the board to another. Where does the knight go, exactly, when it passes through queen or rook or pawn? It exists as pure energy, as the vehicle of the intellect, the assertion of human will. Just as Ilsa and Victor Laszlo fly off into the Moroccan mist, so does the White knight vanish into thin air. The standard rules of engagement are rendered irrelevant. The vanishing is a subtle, spontaneous extension of the preternatural power the knight has possessed all along. What was Bogart attempting (and failing) to communicate to the receptive viewer of his time? What does the vanishing knight communicate to Bogart's twenty-second century audience? These are the questions I pondered as I drifted off to sleep. When I awoke the next morning I believed in God.

* * *

The White Knight

La Belle Aurore: the name of the café Rick Blaine leaves behind in occupied France when he flees to Casablanca. The beautiful dawn. The silhouette of the name cast by Parisian sunlight. On the other side of the window, Sam plays "As Time Goes By," Ilsa and Rick sip champagne while German guns rumble in the distance. It was raining when I awoke on the morning of February 18th, 2105. I had never thought very much about God before. My life's work was dedicated to a secular aspect of an overwhelmingly secular society. Nevertheless, when I woke up that morning I was struck with awe and humility. I suddenly possessed a firm belief in a transcendent, omniscient, omnipresent Supreme Being. I had no proof that a God existed, but I had utter faith that this was indeed the case. I did not know what my belief meant or where it came from. My parents were atheists raised by atheist parents who came from agnostics before them. There are still believers in 2105. They constitute a fringe minority, a dwindling assortment of fragmented religious sects. I have never had an interest in their faith-communities or their anachronistic, twenty-first century theologies. I have never had any friends who believed in God. There is Ahmed from the Faculty of Astro-biology, with whom I occasionally play raquetball. Someone once mentioned in the locker room, derisively, that he is Muslim. But we have never discussed religion. No one ever does.

There is one reference to God in *Casablanca*. It occurs in the note Rick receives before he boards the train.

> *I cannot go with you or ever see you again.*
> *You must not ask why. Go my darling*
> *and God bless you.*

God bless you. This, if anything, is my most meaningful point of reference to the Divine. Ilsa's note to Rick beseeches blind faith, asking of Rick's love what that love makes hardest to give. Ingrid Bergman has an imploring way of looking at her leading men; there is in her eyes an almost desperate devotion.

At first I tried to set my absurd faith aside and get on with my work. I treated my belief much as I would a head cold or a hangover. I took an Aspirin, went to bed early and drank plenty of fluids. Otherwise, I persevered with my research, marked assignments, and played racquetball. But there was no longer satisfaction in these pursuits. My faith persisted. It was not limited to moments of idleness, but was with me in my dreams and in my waking thoughts and in every action I performed. I was no longer content. So I tried a different approach. I devoted more time to my research than ever before, attempting to eliminate all extraneous concerns from my daily routine. I told myself I would complete my dissertation by the end of the summer. But the more I threw myself into my work, the more my faith flourished. I saw God in everything around me. My work, along with everything else in my life, was superceded by my perfect knowledge of God's being.

One night, as I lay in bed with Cynthia, slightly inebriated and unable to manifest my affections, I confided my belief quite spontaneously.

"Cynthia, I believe in God."

"What do you mean?" she asked, of course, and so I explained as best I could, including an account of the note that Ilsa writes to Rick.

"Oh Frank, darling, you're such a sentimental retrophile."

"Well what about you, Cynthia? Your master's thesis is on Audrey Hepburn's wardrobe."

"That's different," she said. "That's historical."

* * *

The White Knight

My belief continued to preoccupy me. On the afternoon of April 5th it was raining again and I was trying desperately to make some headway with my dissertation. I attempted to watch *The Maltese Falcon* and turned it off halfway through. Bogart bored me. I opened a musty mid-twentieth century book of chess strategy I had read countless times before and turned to the chapter on end-game theory. I'm not sure exactly what I was looking for. I suppose I was attempting to understand the appeal my research once held for me. It was at the top of the chapter's first page that I found the quote from Alexander Alekhine, World Chess Champion, 1927 to 1935, 1937 to 1946: "Chess will be the master of us all."

I knew what I had to do. I would play chess.

One of the most intriguing precepts of chess-metaphor theory is that there are more possible games of chess, up to move twenty-five, than there are atoms in the universe. Mid-game play as executed by two grand-masters can be so complex as to appear entirely arbitrary to a layman, or even to an attentive amateur, familiar with basic strategy. It is no coincidence that chess fell out of fashion at the same time as the major world religions. By the early twenty-first century computers started routinely defeating world champions in tournament play, beginning with Kasparov's loss to IBM's *Deep Blue* in 1997. As computers came to dominate at the world championship level, they began competing against each other. It was at this point they succumbed to the same haughtiness, paranoia and anti-Semitic posturing as Bobby Fischer did in the mid-1970s. Soon after, computers stopped playing against one another with any degree of seriousness, and for the most part, humans followed their lead. But the solar system is large enough that there are still people playing, mostly former Eastern Europeans who emigrated to the moons of Jupiter after Chernobyl III.

In a Mist

I have decided to make the move from chess theory to chess practice. It has become my way to convene with the infinite. I have submitted to chess with all the piety of a supplicating monk. I spend as many hours as possible at the board, honing my strategy and technique. Of course I know my limitations. I do not aspire to master or grandmaster status, but to expert ranking, the same held by Humphrey Bogart when he died at fifty-eight of cancer of the esophagus. I continue my work as a teaching assistant, so that I may save enough to travel to Jupiter's moons. There I may learn from and eventually compete against the greatest living chess players and upon my return I will no longer lose to Cynthia. I always felt a certain inexplicable affinity for Fyodor, the Russian bartender at Rick's Café in *Casablanca*. Now I understand, and as a result I have decided to drink vodka exclusively from now on. I was just off the mark before, but I have finally found my way. I am a believer.

The Flank and Spur

It was mid-April and streams cut beneath soiled banks of snow and ran along street-side curbs into storm drains. Isaac stepped carefully to keep the mud from his polished boots. When he arrived it was still early and the bar was almost empty. An acoustic guitar, a bass guitar and a lap-steel plugged into an amplifier rested on stage in front of a drum set. Isaac recognized the front man and lap-steel player seated on stools at the bar, their backs turned to the door. The bartender nodded to Isaac and Isaac nodded and removed his hat. He took off his sheepskin coat and situated himself against a wall without windows so as best to observe the stage and the other side of the room, where most of the patrons would sit. He sat down at a high, sturdy wooden table, choosing a place with a glass ashtray though he had not smoked a cigarette in almost twenty years. He sat for a moment and observed the quiet room. An older woman he recognized and a haggard-looking man he did not were playing slot machines at the back. There was worn green carpet beneath his boots and a scuffed hardwood surface serving as a dance floor. The stage was low, no more than a foot off the floor, and crowded with instruments and amplifiers. On the far side of the room there were small square-paned windows between wine-coloured curtains. A grey-haired waitress greeted Isaac by name and brought him a half-pint glass and a pitcher of pale draft. When she offered him a menu he smiled and declined. He filled his glass and wondered whether the girl would come that afternoon.

It would be two years that July since he first saw her. Though he did not know precisely he put her between the ages of twenty and twenty-five. Once or twice a month she would come and sit on the opposite side of the room with other men and women of her approximate age. Isaac found it curious that the young women outnumbered the young men. He could not fathom that these men would let the women who sat at their table pay for their own drinks. If he could not help but think of these young women as girls, surely the men in their company were no more than boys. He knew that the man he was several decades ago would have felt differently about the girl than he felt now. He could approximate the time, some twenty years ago, when the change in him had occurred. It happened around the same time that women stopped thinking of him as a handsome or desirable man. He watched now as the front man and the lap-steel player took the stage and tuned their instruments and spoke of key signatures and song titles. Eventually they were joined by the others and performed Hank Williams's rendition of "Lovesick Blues," the tune with which they always began.

This was the time Isaac most enjoyed, the afternoon in its potential and him left to contemplate what may transpire. He knew some other old-time regulars would eventually approach him and join his table, another old man, or an aging couple with which he was acquainted. They would laugh at the front man's swagger and his banter and applaud solos and if someone were to sit in for a number, this would be occasion for further applause. They might share a pitcher, speak of the weather or the milestones of grandchildren and if wallet-sized photographs were produced, Isaac would examine them for evidence of bloodline and personality. Together they would look with approval at the young couples on the dance floor, or eye the older ones and wink. To exercise his independence Isaac would rise on occasion and make his way to the slots, methodically inserting quarters until he reached his three dollar limit. He would return then to the table with a sense of self-control he wished he might have been able to exercise with as little effort in other affairs.

Gradually the bar began to fill. Isaac looked back toward the entrance as a woman his age entered, followed by a man who had held the door for her. The two were dressed in western shirts with matching embroidery. When they saw Isaac they waved to him but did not approach. They sat down behind him, at the back of the room, and the man went off to the bar and when the woman saw Isaac looking in her direction she winked at him.

"You sly old devil," said a familiar voice and Isaac turned and Lloyd grinned at him. Lloyd's greying beard was newly trimmed. He wore a navy-issue sweater with a collared shirt underneath and a brand new ball cap perched on the crown of his head. Isaac greeted his old acquaintance and shook his outstretched, calloused hand and Lloyd set the half-pint in his other hand on the table and sat down next to Isaac without being asked. Isaac turned to face the stage and it was then he saw that the girl had arrived and was sitting in a crowd of young people on the other side of the room.

On a crowded afternoon the previous fall, when the young people were more numerous, someone had introduced him to the girl and her party. Isaac had spoken to her twice. She had remembered his name from the first of these occasions and had smiled at him, warmly, on the second.

By all signs she was unmarried, which was not uncommon, but which troubled him nevertheless. He did not know whether this caused the same concern in her as it did in him. He knew only that the girl wore horn-rimmed glasses, spoke softly, held her hands in her lap when she sat, curtsied to her partner as a song ended, never dancing with the same partner twice in a row. Though she could waltz, she favoured the two-step and the jive, shied from that formless dance in which partners press closely together, sway to ballads and whisper in one another's ear. When she danced with a young man who was not her equal on the floor, Isaac had seen her discreetly take the lead. When the girl would be asked to dance by another man, no matter Isaac's knowledge of him or his opinion as to the man's moral character, Isaac would feel a strangely bitter sense of relief, of things being as they should.

When she danced and the burden of her would lift from Isaac's thoughts, or at other times, his mind at ease, he would think then of his older brother. It was not that he still mourned Roland or missed him particularly, but strangely his brother had come to inhabit his thoughts in a way he never had while living. Isaac attributed this to the sentimentality of old age. Roland, dead some nine years now, had never learned to speak. After their mother passed on he had spent the last two decades of his life in a home in a neighbouring town. In the early years Isaac had visited. He would sit at the table where Roland was served his meals and watch his brother take infrequent sips from an endless cup of decaf. Roland would smile mysteriously at these times, glancing at him with something Isaac chose to interpret as the acknowledgment of a common origin. As the years passed these glances grew less meaningful and when recognition gave way entirely to indifference, Isaac stopped visiting. He felt relief at this, for after nine years he could no longer tolerate the way in which his brother was addressed by the staff of the home, well-intentioned caregivers who spoke to a man twice their age as if he were a child. Though he had never wiped himself, nor bathed of his own volition, nor so much as danced with a woman, Isaac knew that Roland was not a child in his old age if he had ever been one. He knew Roland would have lived a much different life had he been given the opportunity, and Isaac respected him for who he might have been.

He had long come to accept that his brother could not be held accountable as others were held accountable. This acceptance was bound up inextricably with an image of the kitchen table overturned, warm red smeared on the fainter red and white of his mother's gingham apron. He could not now ascertain if this had been blood or the remains of an upset rhubarb pie, for each had precedent and each was equally calamitous in Isaac's childhood recollection. As a grown man he could not accept that Roland was deemed a child and spoken to as such. He knew his brother had endured fifty-some odd post-pubescent years of masculine urges and scoldings and the erratic nocturnal manifestations of frustrated desire. Isaac at least had work—long stretches of highway with predetermined destinations, physical and mental exhaustion, the repetition of tiresome but nevertheless necessary and even useful tasks. This among other pastimes, even on occasion the companionship of women, and always a few friends, acquaintances, who if they did not understand the nature of his reticence, spoke to him at least in the terms of their common adulthood, of time spent working, longing and sometimes being satisfied.

For eleven years before Roland's passing, all that remained of the place in Isaac's life once occupied by his brother was a birthday card, signed with his brother's name by the staff of the home, accompanied by a gift certificate for a chain of coffee shops Isaac had not patronized since he quit smoking. These tokens, and memories of a childhood shared with his brother, would come upon him at times when he was otherwise at ease. He had long forgotten the date of his brother's birth and could not bring himself to ask. Out of a steadfast sense of obligation that ended only with Roland's death, he would reciprocate his birthday card with a card for his brother at Christmas. His brother had always taken some pleasure in music. And the card would, on better years, be accompanied by a recording of something he hoped that Roland might enjoy.

Isaac himself sought out music on AM radios and in bars. He would tap his foot inaudibly, could mouth the words to hundreds of songs so long as they played, could hum something resembling the tunes to as many though he had never owned a record. If he heard a melody he had not heard in years, he would feel the pleasure of recognition, as if chancing upon an old acquaintance in a motel bar or walking the streets of a distant town from a favourable time in his past. He could dance with a confidence that came from a certain degree of practice, beginning with a long ago series of afternoon lessons given by a red-haired sitter in the years when his mother worked and his father was at war. He could remember dancing with this girl, who was years older and a head taller. He could recall the feel of his hand on the back of the girl's cotton print dress, though he could not remember the names of the songs to which they had danced or who sang them. Given the presence of a jukebox in a truck stop or an all-night diner he would make selections at random or ask an idle waitress to choose her favourite tune. In 1959, at the suggestion of a girl he was seeing at the time, he had taken to styling his hair in the pompadour style of Elvis Presley. It suited him and he saw no reason to change and though his hair had since grown pale and thin to the degree that what remained was hardly worth the effort, he still kept a fine-toothed comb in a brown leather sheaf in his back pocket so that he might maintain this ghost of youthful vanity.

Among the young men who would frequent the Flank and Spur on Sunday afternoons was one who wore his hair in the same style and would sit in the company of the girl. Isaac noted that this young man took to the floor on occasion, but he could not determine whether his pomaded hair and his mother-of-pearl button-down shirts tucked into dark pressed denims gave him any particular success with women. If the young man had been a slightly better dancer, if Isaac had been able to discern in him something of character, he might have wished him to court the girl. On two separate occasions he had noticed an alarming vacancy come over the young man when he had too much to drink. This was upsetting given his youth, and did not bode well for when true hardship befell him. The girl had nothing of the boy's showiness, nor the harshness of appearance of some of the other young people. She did not seem to affect the style of another era and yet her long plaid skirt and her cream-coloured sweater set her apart from the time in which she lived. There were colleges and universities in the city and he heard the other regulars talk to the young people of programs and degrees. He did not know whether the girl was a student. When the band quit, she would leave, alone, or with a group of her companions. Isaac had overheard once that she had to get up early on Monday mornings though he knew not why this was the case.

His thoughts were interrupted as an old woman approached their table, beaming at Lloyd, her wrinkled face framed in tight, white ringlets. She bore a wicker basket filled with tickets, a can with a slot in its lid and a hand-written label that read *Children's Charity Hospital 50/50*.

In a Mist

Isaac knew that Sheila was nearly eighty, though he would not have believed her to be so old if she had not told him herself. She was forthright with her age having lived long enough so that the number of her years was not an embarrassment, but a point of pride. Lloyd reached into his front pocket and retrieved a five dollar bill and folded it and slid it through the slot in the can. Sheila took a roll of tickets from the pocket of her cardigan and counted them. She felt each perforation with the tips of her fingers as if she could not trust her eyes.

"Good luck," she said to Lloyd, and placed his tickets on the table and placed their mates in the wicker basket.

"I'll need it," he said and lifted his glass to his lips and turned back toward the stage.

Isaac asked for his usual two dollar's worth and she presented him with four tickets, laying her hands upon his. He might have thought she was flirting had he not known she favoured the company of his roommate, Aubrey, who had stopped coming to the Flank and Spur some months ago for reasons he would not discuss. He folded the tickets and placed them in the breast pocket of his shirt. Her touch left behind the heavy scent of a floral perfume—lilac he supposed, though she had moved on to the far side of the room before he thought to ask.

Isaac watched as an unshaven man of thirty years or slightly more, in cowboy boots and a black t-shirt with a motorcycle on the front approached the girl and asked her to dance. She agreed, hesitantly, and the two jived to a Carl Perkins tune. When the song ended the man's hand remained on the girl's arm. With his other hand he gestured to the empty stools at the bar. The girl forced a smile, shook her head. The man released her arm, muttered something and walked away. It occurred to Isaac then that the crowd was drinking more than usual, more than the occasion called for, as sometimes happened on Sundays that followed the receipt of government cheques. The pitcher on their table was empty and Isaac felt the strain in his bladder. He turned to Lloyd and excused himself and got up and made his way across the room. At least one man had emptied the contents of his stomach in a rest room stall and the talk at the urinals was exclusively of women and of desire for them. After he had urinated Isaac went to the sink and as he washed his hands and found himself standing next to the man in the motorcycle t-shirt. The man ran his hands through his dark, close-cropped hair and examined his teeth in the mirror.

"I don't intend on leaving this bar alone," the man said. "I intend on having some company."

Isaac was uncertain whether the comment was addressed to him. He turned off the faucet and reached toward the paper towel dispenser before he saw that it was empty. He shook the water from his hands and then wiped them on the back of his pants. The man in the t-shirt turned to him.

"You know what I'm talking about old-timer. I've been watching you," he said.

Isaac turned and walked out of the washroom without acknowledging the man. When he got back to the table the empty pitcher had been replaced by a full one, his glass filled. He turned to thank Lloyd but the band counted in an upbeat tune and Lloyd suddenly rose to his feet and went to the table at the back of the room and said something to the man seated there. The man nodded his assent and Lloyd smiled and extended his hand to the man's wife who accompanied him to the dance floor. He looked at Isaac and called out something as they passed but Isaac could not hear him over the sound of the band. Before Isaac could empty his glass he had grown tired of the taste of the draft and the bitter feeling of it in his throat. He watched as a man not quite as old as him did his best to charm two younger women at a neighbouring table. The song ended and Lloyd escorted the woman back to her seat and pulled up a chair and joined in conversation with her and her husband. The man in the motorcycle t-shirt sat at the bar behind them. Isaac watched as he lifted a shot glass of whiskey to his lips, and then another, as if he had abandoned his earlier intention in favour of a less ambitious pursuit.

There was an intermission and the front man of the band, perhaps twenty years younger than Isaac, went over to the other side of the room and seated himself next to the girl. The front man was solid and brazen in a leather vest and western tie, a short man, the same the height as the girl. He was too old for her but he was a talker and a dancer when the opportunity allowed. Isaac had tried to like the man for years and had failed. Now the front man said something and the showy young man laughed and the others laughed and the girl laughed as well. She wore her hair down to her slender shoulders and when she turned her head Isaac noticed the peculiar blonde streak behind her left ear. It did not seem natural and he wondered what had brought her to style it in that way.

The streak reminded him of one seen in his childhood. A thunderstorm had passed through the lowland where his family lived and left a blackout in its wake. A neighbour of half a mile's distance, a lineman, was sent to repair the line after the storm had passed and an unlikely surge had killed him instantly. Then came rumours and sightings of a sudden milk-white streak through the raven hair of a woman from town, a distant cousin of Isaac's mother. Grief arising from trauma was known to cause such signs and this would have been of little consequence had the young woman been the widow of the deceased and not her sister. Those close to the widow spoke of her grief and the strange transference of its physical manifestation. Others speculated as to the true reason for the mark, observing that the accident had not brought the sisters closer but caused a rift to grow between them. More peculiar was that the mark was said to stretch from root to tip though it appeared only days after the storm had blown out to sea and dissipated somewhere over the Atlantic.

The streak in the girl's hair was a softer flaxen upon chestnut brown. Though Isaac was not predisposed to affectation he found himself drawn to this mark in her shoulder-length hair. He was not so old that he could not imagine that hair upon the pillow of his ancient bachelor's bed. And yet he was long resigned to such yearnings becoming nothing more. If not steady companionship or wealth, he had his faculties and seven decades very little of which he was ashamed. A lapse in the control of his bowels a year previous had shaken him—made him question the value of his existence as it took from him what dignity he once possessed. He had learned then that certain skills acquired in youth matter more than those acquired later on. With the help of a specialist and a prescription this hateful time had passed, miraculously, leaving him content to live and to think about the girl for some time to come.

Whether it was right for the girl to have such a place in his thoughts was not a question that vexed him as it might once have. He had come to know himself and those appetites that must be sated and those that must be dulled through deception as a man starving fills his belly with water from a clear stream until he is fed or until he dies. So long as he respected the limits of his tolerance for drink he would maintain control. He wondered whether he would think of her differently if she were married, if she were the wife of another man, a man who worked and whose children she bore? Isaac had known no children of his own, nor nieces or nephews, his parents having forgone attempts at further progeny after one child slow and silent and another nearly silent. He knew he was old and possessed of an inward pride and sensibility that many men lacked. He could have asked her to dance and it could have been no different, for those who witnessed, from an elderly man asking a young bride to dance at her wedding, a daughter, the daughter of a brother, of a childhood acquaintance, the daughter of a man he knew but for whom he did not care. He knew she might turn him down, or she might accept out of pity. He did not think it foolish for a boy or a young man or woman to fear. He wondered whether this was the case for a man of his years who knows better what he stood to lose and how easily it might be lost.

Mercifully the intermission ended and the dance floor became crowded once more so that he could only see across the room for brief intervals between songs. Lloyd returned to the table and emptied the rest of the pitcher into his own glass and looked at Isaac and then toward the stage. The front man, now loose and confident with drink, made no attempt to disguise the lewdness of his banter. Lloyd leaned in toward Isaac and in an air of confidence he stated as plain and scientific fact it was impossible to croon and strum a guitar and dance with a woman at one and the same time. Isaac nodded his assent and though he knew the remark was intended as a jest he took comfort in it still. He did not think himself necessarily qualified to pass judgement, but he thought maybe the band was not quite as good as it might be, that maybe they did not take the care that they should because they had played there for at least ten years and no one was going to deny them their complimentary refreshment or their modest take. He had never strummed a guitar nor had he ever had a sincere desire to do so, and the act struck him as garnering more attention than it deserved. The girl danced several times,

The Flank and Spur

once with a much older man, and Isaac took pleasure in the grace of her movement and the fact that she was dancing. He knew only a few numbers remained, maybe two or three, before the band said goodnight and packed it in and if he was going to ask the girl he could not afford to wait. Instead he asked Lloyd for a cigarette and a light. The cigarette between his lips, Isaac held Lloyd's Zippo to its tip, turned its wheel and inhaled deeply. A wave of nausea washed over him. He was loath to waste even a cigarette, but he extinguished it in the ashtray as he struggled for his breath. Lloyd looked up at him, chuckled, and turned his attention to the band. Isaac took the tickets for the 50/50 draw from his breast pocket and laid them on the pack of cigarettes next to the empty pitcher, having decided to leave before the band could finish. He put on his hat and his coat, worked his way through the crowd, not acknowledging anyone at all. In protest of he knew not what exactly he headed to the door and was thwarted as the band concluded their number and bid the crowd goodnight. He made it out into the April gloom before the applause had subsided but this did not console him. He cursed loudly and made his way across the lot indifferent to the mud that soiled his spit-polished boots as the door banged after him. His utterance did not meet its mark and he uttered a second livid invective against all circumstance. This time he was overheard by a dark-complexioned man who emerged from the shadows of the building wearing a thin and soiled nylon jacket bearing some illegible logo With an earnestness that matched that of Isaac's declaration the man asked him for nothing less than a whole dollar. Isaac knew he had the means and that he had squandered many times this in the hours just passed in the bar. He said nothing to the man and responded with a gesture that indicated his unwillingness to comply. The man wished him a good night in a manner if not sincere than

In a Mist

with an air of sincerity so polished and infinitely rehearsed and natural-seeming in its execution that Isaac was almost convinced the man was not trying to manipulate him, a feeling he had experienced countless times before when he had declined to give up his spare change. He felt this for an instant and then it passed and for whatever reason he decided to take the man and his gesture at face value and reciprocated the expression of good will. Isaac walked on into the night. He felt that the air was cold and damp but he did not feel the bite of it.

Aubrey was at home watching a movie and greeted Isaac without looking up. Isaac wanted to be alone but he took off his boots and his coat and hat and laid his coat on the arm of the chesterfield and sat down. He contemplated the indignity of having to share a flat with another man at his age, even one as benign as Aubrey. Then he felt ashamed when Aubrey asked him if he wanted something to eat. Aubrey got up and went into the kitchen and as Isaac watched the movie he could hear him moving around. The movie was sentimental, maudlin even in the manner of Sunday night made-for-TV movies, about a middle-aged woman who worked as an orderly in a maternity ward and her retarded sister. Isaac felt his eyes begin to water and by the time Aubrey returned he had fought his tears and had won. Aubrey set down two plates of eggs and peameal bacon and walked out and came back again with a ketchup bottle and two mugs of milkless tea. Isaac thanked him and when Aubrey, who had once served as a cabin boy for a Vice-Admiral, asked him how it was tonight, Isaac said it was the same as always. The two men watched the movie in silence and ate their supper. Sometime between finishing his eggs and the rolling of the credits Aubrey nodded off. Isaac turned off the television and sat in the near-dark for some time. Eventually he picked up the plates and the mugs and brought them to the kitchen and put them in the sink and put the ketchup bottle in the refrigerator. He filled a glass with water from the tap and took an Aspirin from the bottle in the cabinet over the sink. He stood in the living room drinking the water. Snowflakes began to fall in the light of the street lamp outside the second story window. He put the glass in the kitchen sink on top of the plates and went into Aubrey's room and took a blanket from the unmade bed and when he lay it over Aubrey, Aubrey turned over on his side and murmured in his sleep. Then Isaac went into his own room and took off his socks, unbuttoned his shirt, unbuckled his belt and took off his pants and placed them over a chair in the corner of the room. He got under the blankets of his bed. He thought about the girl for only a moment. Before he fell asleep he speculated, not with indifference, as to his waking in the morning.

The Crow's Nest

She broke a porcelain cup that morning as she left for class, knocking it over with her knapsack as she stormed out of the kitchen. English Breakfast tea spilled over the counter and onto the floor Richard had just scrubbed the day before.

"For Christ's sakes, Laura."

"I'm late."

She pushed past him and he grabbed her bare arm and blocked her path, but then let go and stepped aside when he saw the look in her eye. A moment later he heard her running down the stairs and then the sound of the door as it slammed.

After he wiped up the tea and swept the shards of porcelain into the garbage he poured himself a glass of water and walked out onto the second story balcony in his bare feet. There were no clouds in the sky. Oak and maple leaves riddled with caterpillar holes hung limply in the heat. Bags and cans of trash lined the residential street below. A bearded man in a tracksuit stood behind an empty shopping cart, prodding a bulging bag with a cane. He said something to himself, rested the cane inside the cart and started pushing it, the wheels rattling over the cracks in the sidewalk. Students headed down the street in the opposite direction, toward the university.

The trouble had begun in March when Richard's grandmother passed away. He had been writing all along, bartending four nights a week, spending the afternoons in his study before he went to work and writing for a few hours on his days off. But he was sick of the job and as soon as he got word of the inheritance he knew he'd quit and write full-time. His grandmother had always been supportive of his writing and he liked to think she'd approve of this decision. She hadn't left him a lot of money but he figured it should last him almost a year if he spent it wisely.

"Give it time," Laura had said at first. "It takes time to adjust to a new routine." But by the time she went back to school in the third week of August things still hadn't improved. He hadn't finished anything since he'd quit and now the inheritance was more than half gone. He went inside and sat at his desk in the walk-in closet off their bedroom. The closet had been one of the reasons they had decided on the place when they moved in together the year before. He'd insisted on having a study but they hadn't been able to afford an extra room. The closet was just big enough for his desk and chair. When Laura was studying at home she would lie on the bed with her textbooks and notes and listen to the classical station on the radio. He would close the door and work at his desk with earplugs in his ears. When they first moved in she had once asked to use his desk to write a paper but he had refused, claiming that he needed the space to concentrate and that she was capable of working anywhere. She had shrugged and accepted this, setting up her laptop on the kitchen table. Occasionally, when he'd come home from work, he'd sit at his desk and write something that had been on the back of his mind as he pulled pints and wiped down tables. He would have overheard a conversation. Someone would tell a peculiar story or confess an infidelity and he would do his best to remember the details so he could write them down as soon as he got home. He'd sit in the closet with the door closed, writing by the light of his desk lamp while Laura lay asleep in the adjoining room. It was nights like these that made his job tolerable. But they did not happen very often. Most of time he couldn't stand O'Grady's or the business majors who drank there. He told himself that the place was stifling his creativity, that he'd quit as soon as possible. He would often have a drink with the staff after closing, usually four or five on Saturdays when his workweek ended, and when he sat down to write on Sunday afternoons he was fuzzy-headed and struggled to work out of the haze.

The last thing he'd finished before he quit O'Grady's was the eulogy he'd written for his grandmother. His mother had insisted he read at the funeral. It had been one of the hardest things he'd ever done. He started a dozen drafts without getting anywhere. Finally he decided on writing his earliest memories of his grandmother. Sitting on her lap after she'd read him a story, watching her cat on the windowsill—a kitten then—swat houseflies out of the air. His grandmother standing in her garden with a red kerchief in her hair, picking a cucumber off the vine, showing him how to rinse it with the garden hose, smoothing off the tiny green spikes with her thumb. Everyone told him that the eulogy had been moving, that he'd surpassed their expectations. His degree in English literature, all the hours spent sitting in libraries, scribbling away in walk-in closets were justified to his family by this performance. But in his own eyes he had failed to convey how he felt about his grandmother. Writing the eulogy had only frustrated him, made him doubt his ability to do what was most important to him. Now, sitting at his desk six months later, he admitted to himself that the eulogy had made him realize how much his grandmother had meant to him, even if he hadn't been able to express his emotions. He was saddened by the fact that he had never thought to write anything about her while she was alive. This gave him an idea.

Laura was the most important person in my life. We never talked about it openly, but we both assumed that we would spend the rest of our lives together. She was pragmatic, rational, systematic. But also compassionate, and optimistic. More so than I. We were very different. But we seemed to complement one another. She was the perfect companion for someone like me. I knew this at one point but gradually I began to forget. I withdrew into myself. She realized what I was doing before I did and she reacted with anger. This only caused me to draw further away from her. The day she died we were more distant from one another than we had ever been before.

He tore the page out of his notebook, crumpled it up and threw it in the wastebin. After staring at the notebook for some time he considered retrieving the page and continuing. But he thought better of it. He got up from his desk and walked out of the room. He could not bear the thought of staying in the apartment alone all afternoon, waiting for her to come home. He went to the hallway closet and took out a short sleeved shirt and put it on over his sleeveless undershirt. He sat down on the bench in the hallway and put on socks and shoes, pausing after he tied the lace of the right shoe, wondering where he would go. He considered the university library but he could not stand the presence of students and did not want to risk running into her. He locked the door, descended the stairs and decided to head north. The air was heavy with the odor of garbage at the curbs. At the end of the block he watched a mangy tabby retreat from a torn bag of trash toward the underside of a front step, something dark and limp hanging from its mouth.

When he passed the convenience store at the end of the next block he left his neighbourhood behind. Victorian homes converted into student flats gave way to identical row houses, and then a stretch of squat brick tenements where there were no trees lining the street to provide shade. He took a handkerchief from his back pocket and dabbed the sweat from his forehead. In front of one of the tenements two young girls sat on overturned milk crates behind a folding table. They wore matching one-piece pink and yellow bathing suits and cotton baseball caps and their skin was tanned a dark brown. There was a clear plastic pitcher on the table, Styrofoam cups, and cans of soda glinting in the sun.

"Lemonade. Seventy five cents. Pop for a dollar," said the older of the two girls, eyeing him. She fidgeted, twisted on her milk crate, the palms of her hands resting beside her slender thighs. Her fingers drummed the side of the milk crate, as if keeping time to a tune only she could hear. The younger girl looked up at him silently. Richard reached into his empty front pocket.

"Do you have change for a five?" he asked.

"Umm . . ." said the fidgeting girl, her smile vanishing.

"That's alright," he said. "You should put that soda in a cooler."

"The lemonade's cold," said the older girl. He could see half-melted ice cubes floating in the pitcher of cloudy white liquid.

"I'll get change." She jumped up and ran toward the building, her flip flops slapping against the asphalt. He looked down at the younger girl and smiled. She looked up at him with two fingers in her mouth. He did not want to stand in the sun and wait for her companion to return.

"You picked a good day for selling lemonade," he said. "I wish you luck."

In a Mist

Soon after he passed between a series of car lots, the pristine vehicles reflecting heat and light off their polished glass and chrome. A balding salesman in a dark green suit shielded his eyes with a clipboard, making his way between a row of brightly coloured Korean compacts toward the air conditioned showroom. It occurred to Richard that he'd have to walk back as far as he'd come, but he felt compelled to keep going. Beyond the car lots lay a commercial zone full of sprawling factory outlets and aluminium-sided warehouses with loading bays for tractor trailers. In the distance he could make out the towering cranes of a container pier and the glimmer of sunlight on the ocean. Across an empty parking lot stood a squat building with pale blue vinyl siding and a patio of varnished wood, empty of patrons. As he approached he could read the words "Crow's Nest" arched in yellow letters around a ship's wheel on the sign that hung from the side of the building. He wasn't sure if it would be open but there were two cars parked out front and he decided to give it a try. An air conditioner rested in an open window next to the door. There was a damp stain on the pavement directly beneath it where water dripped steadily, evaporating almost instantly in the sun.

He opened the front door and the cool air enveloped him. He ran his hands over his bare arms and felt goose bumps. It took a moment for his eyes to adjust to the dim light of the bar. A few empty wooden tables and video lottery terminals filled the back of the room. On the back wall hung a wooden ship's wheel draped with plastic pennants advertising beer. There was a television with the volume turned down mounted over the bar. A man sat at the far end of the bar and another man stood behind. When he entered they stopped talking to one another and turned toward the door. Richard exchanged nods with both men and sat on a stool halfway down the bar so that he could turn to see the television screen. The bartender had a crewcut and a goatee and wore a Boston Bruins t-shirt tucked into his faded jeans. The man who sat at the bar was older and heavier with thick eyebrows and greying hair. He wore a dark red flannel shirt with the top two buttons undone and the sleeves rolled up, tawny work boots and brown work pants with a western-style belt. A pint glass half full of draft rested on the bar in front of him. The air conditioner hummed.

"What can I get you?" asked the bartender.

"Scotch please," said Richard. "And a glass of water." The bartender thumped the bar once with his fingers and turned to the shelf of spirits. Above the liquor bottles was a second shelf full of sports trophies: gilded figures of hockey players blanketed in a thin film of dust.

The bartender stood with his back to Richard and looked over the selection, his hand suspended in the air before the bottles. He muttered something, chose a bottle of Irish whiskey, measured an ounce in a shot glass and poured it into a tumbler. He rested the glass in front of Richard on a cardboard coaster, then ran the tap for several seconds before filling a water glass.

Richard said nothing and lifted the whiskey glass to his lips. He chased the whiskey with a sip of water and turned his attention to the television. An image of a supersonic jet filled the screen and then a razor blade. An athletic, bare-chested man ran the tips of his fingers along his cleanly shaven jaw.

"Work around here?" asked the man seated at the bar.

"No, I don't." Richard turned to face him.

"Funny place to come on your afternoon off," said the man. Richard noticed a slight lilt in his speech. The bartender cleared his throat.

"Quit bothering the customers, Lloyd," he said, winking at Richard.

"It's true though," said Lloyd. "Wouldn't catch me anywhere near this place if I didn't work down the street." He drank from his beer. "You're looking for work then," Lloyd said to Richard. "You can tell when a man's been out of work for a while."

"Can you now," said the bartender.

"No shame in it. Being out of a job," said Lloyd.

The bartender counted a stack of bills into the till.

"Need any help around here, Stu?" asked Lloyd. Stu looked at Lloyd, then made a show of looking around the room.

"Think I got it under control," he said, focusing his attention back on the till. Lloyd leaned in over the bar.

"Might try hiring a young fella to work evenings. Just might get some females in here then. Be good for business." Stu ignored him and Lloyd turned to Richard. "You don't want to work in a place like this anyway. Depressing."

Stu paused for a second, looked up at Lloyd. Richard finished his whiskey.

"Another?" asked Stu.

"I'm good for now." Richard took another swallow of water, then took out his wallet and laid a five dollar bill on the counter. Lloyd set his empty pint glass on the bar.

"Guess I'd better head home," he said.

"You don't intend to get started on that job this afternoon?" asked Stu.

"In this heat?" said Lloyd. "I know better."

"Maybe this young fella doesn't," said Stu.

"What I was thinking," said Lloyd.

* * *

The vinyl upholstery of Lloyd's Olds 88 clung to the bare skin of Richard's arms. A cardboard pine tree hung from the rear view mirror, filling the air with its chemical fragrance. They rolled down the windows and when they got on the highway the breeze began to cool the car's interior. Lloyd had the radio on low, tuned to a classic country station, and Richard could make out the faint twang of Dolly Parton.

Lloyd had one hand on the wheel and his other arm hung out the open window. A pair of aviator sunglasses obscured his eyes.

"Ever think about heading out west? To find work?" he said.

"Can't say I've given it much thought."

"I've got a son. Jim. Went out that way as soon as he finished high school. Found something right away. Makes good money."

"Glad it worked out for him."

"He had nothing keeping him here though." Lloyd took his eyes from the road and glanced at Richard.

"I won't pretend I don't miss him," said Lloyd. "But you can't blame young people for doing what they have to do." Richard looked out the window at the side of the road.

"No you can't," he said.

"I left Newfoundland for the mainland when I was seventeen."

"Ever been back?"

"Once."

The city limits fell behind them and they approached the trees and lakes beyond.

"Is there a bus that heads back to the city from out this way?" said Richard.

"Closest bus leaves from Fall River. But I wouldn't worry about that if I were you."

Lloyd turned off the highway onto an exit ramp that led to a side road lined with dense forest. They slowed to cross a set of railroad tracks and then pulled into a gravel driveway another few kilometres down the road. The driveway ended in front of a squat wood-shingled house, its brown paint flaking off to reveal patches of dark red paint beneath. There was a small satellite dish mounted on the side of the house and a power line leading back down to the road. Lloyd parked the car beside the rusted body of an old Pontiac station wagon with no tires and no windows. He opened his door and got out and Richard followed. The yard was covered in tall grass that had wilted in the sun. To the left was the dried bed of a pond that had shrunk to the size of a puddle. Past the pond Richard could make out the railroad tracks on a slight embankment about a hundred meters away. Beyond the tracks lay dense evergreen forest.

"I like my privacy," said Lloyd, gesturing beyond the pond. "Those tracks made it a luxury I could afford when I bought this place. Thirty years later and I've almost gotten used to the noise of the trains." He made his way to the back of the house, to a weathered shed built of unpainted slats with a slanted, shingled roof. Between the shed and the house there was a tree stump about half a meter wide, its pale ringed surface chipped and dented. Blocks of firewood were stacked against one side of the shed, reaching almost as high as the taller side of its roof.

"Suppose I should've asked if you ever done this before. Jim used to take care of this. Ever since he was old enough." Lloyd lifted the latch on the shed door, stepped inside and came out carrying a long-handled axe. He rested the axe against the wall of the shed, and set a block of wood on the stump. Richard stepped back.

"Get a good stance, let gravity do the work," said Lloyd, raising the blade of the axe and bringing it down dead-centre on the block. The wood split in two and fell at his feet.

"You'll want boots and gloves." With one hand he sank the blade of the axe into the stump and went off toward the back door of the house. The worst of the day's heat was over but Richard could feel the sweat on his neck and under his arms. He unbuttoned his shirt and hung it on a rusted nail protruding from the doorway of the shed. Then he sat down on the stump and untied his shoes. He wondered whether Lloyd intended to give him the boots he had been wearing on his own feet. But Lloyd came back out a moment later carrying a much older pair with the steel exposed at the toe. His left hand held a pair of leather work gloves and a green mesh ball cap.

"Keep the sun off your head." He held up the cap and Richard could make out the same ship's wheel and yellow lettering he had seen on the sign outside the Crow's Nest. It looked as if it had never been worn.

"Stack it up in the shed once it's split." Lloyd set down the boots and went back toward the house.

The boots were only slightly too big and Richard laced them tightly. He put on the ball cap and the gloves and then set a mid-sized block of wood on the stump as Lloyd had done. He could feel the old man's eyes on him from the doorway of the house as he raised the axe and brought it down, heard him chuckle as he grazed the block and knocked it to the ground. Richard set the block back on the stump, braced himself, raised the axe and brought it down a second time, this time sinking the blade a third of the way into the block. Using the handle of the axe he raised the block as high in the air as his strength would allow and brought it down with a grunt. He lost his footing, stumbling toward the stump as the block split in two, and fell to the ground. He looked back toward the house but Lloyd had gone inside and shut the door. He could hear the sound of the television coming from an open window. Richard's stomach rumbled and he realized he hadn't eaten anything since breakfast.

He worked steadily, gradually improving his technique, increasing his accuracy. He found the work satisfying, taking pleasure in the arc of the axe's blade as it cut through the air, the crack of the dry wood as it split. He could measure his progress as the split wood began to accumulate on the ground before him. Once he established a momentum he found no need to rest. He did not stop even when the handle of the axe began to burn his hands and blisters formed inside the gloves. The steady repetition was mesmerizing, propelling him onward when his mouth dried and his arms began to ache. It was not until he had worked for several hours that he rested the axe against the shed and wiped his forehead with the back of his glove. The shadows had grown and the sound of crickets coming from the grass at the edge of the dried pond had intensified. He heard the train long before he saw it coming. The air horn blared and the wheels sounded against the rails and then it rolled into view, approaching steadily, growing louder and nearer, commanding his attention. The blade of the axe rested against the ground and he leaned his weight on its shaft and stood and watched the blue-grey passenger train as it passed. The faces in its windows appeared to him only as streaks, though he knew they could see him clearly. In his last semester of university he had taken the train to a conference in Moncton. He turned to look at Lloyd's house as the train disappeared from view. He imagined the old man in his bed in the dark of February, awakened for the thousandth time by the passing clamour in the frigid night.

He gathered as many of the split pieces in his arms as he could and carried them into the shed. The air inside was dry and warm and the scent of earth and sawdust and decaying wood made him want to lie down and rest. He set the wood down against the back wall, went out for more and worked until he had filled the far corner of the shed. As he deposited his last load on the earthen floor he noticed something on the side wall. By the thin shafts of sunlight between the slats he could make out a magazine centerfold tacked to a cross-beam. The monochrome print had a silvery sheen and at first he thought its colours had faded with time, but when he saw the figure he knew she had been photographed in black and white. A lithe, young model in sailor shorts dangled over a calm sea, holding onto a ship's rigging with her left hand, waving with her sailor's hat in her right. She had short bangs and dark curls that hung to her shoulders. The nipples of her bare breasts were erect, as if chilled by the ocean breeze. Her left knee was bent as she perched one foot on the bottom of the rigging. Her other long, shapely leg was fully extended, its pointed bare foot poised squarely on the deck. She smiled coyly, her eyes betraying the slightest hint of trepidation at her precarious pose. Richard thought of the men's magazines in his neighbourhood corner store, and could not imagine this sort of expression on the face of the models between their pages. He realized it was most likely not Jim who had hung the photo, but his father. It occurred to Richard that Jim must have seen this photograph every time he filled the wood shed and every time it was emptied in the spring. He wondered what he had thought of this model, whether he had ever mentioned her to his father or shared the old man's evident enthusiasm for her.

When he came out of the shed Lloyd was standing in the doorway of the house.

"Thought you'd gone to sleep in there," he said. "Come have something to drink."

He took the can of orange soda that Lloyd offered him, and was glad to find it ice cold. He drank it quickly while Lloyd appraised the progress he'd made in the unsplit wood stacked outside the shed. When he finished the soda he asked Lloyd for a glass of water. Lloyd took the empty can him from him and came back a moment later with a mug of water. It was lukewarm and tasted slightly of coffee.

"Called the fella from down the road. He's due in for an evening shift. He'll take you back in."

"I appreciate it."

"I'd have you back to finish up some other time, but I figure I'll do it myself once it cools off a little. Keeps me in shape."

Richard nodded. He went to the stump and sat down, untied the boots and put his shoes back on, wondering whether Lloyd regretted hiring him. He took the boots and the hat back up to the house. As he rapped on the screen door he could smell the odour of frying fish.

Lloyd opened the door, took a billfold from his front pocket, peeled off a crisp fifty and handed it to Richard.

"Don't spend it all at the Crow's Nest."

Richard put the bill in his wallet and accepted Lloyd's outstretched hand.

"I'm grateful for the work."

"Better head down to the road," said Lloyd. "He won't drive up. You'll be lucky if he slows down long enough for you to open the door."

"Sure. Take care, Lloyd." Richard had walked halfway down the drive when Lloyd called out.

"You're forgetting something."

He turned to see Lloyd standing by the shed. Lloyd held the axe in his hands and Richard realized he had forgotten to put it away. Richard walked back toward the shed, unsure of what was expected of him. Lloyd gripped the axe handle, pointed toward the door of the shed with its shaft, where Richard's shirt hung on a nail. Richard grabbed the shirt and hurried back toward the road.

"Don't worry," Lloyd called out. "Things will turn around

for you. Stick to your guns."

Richard waved once, and turned to watch the road. He heard the screen door bang at the back of the house. A few minutes later an ancient grey Chevrolet pickup approached in the distance and came to a stop a few feet from where Richard stood.

Richard opened the door, climbed onto the running board and into the cab. The man behind the wheel had a dark moustache, wore a suit of navy blue work clothes and a tweed driver's cap. The brim's shadow fell on his face and Richard couldn't tell if the man was forty years old or sixty or something in between. A metal lunch pail and a Thermos rested on the seat beside him.

"Evening," said Richard.

"I'll drop you uptown," said the man.

"Fine by me," said Richard, and closed the door.

The cab of the truck was air conditioned and the windows rolled up. The two men drove in silence, neither making any attempt at conversation. Richard looked out the window at trees and then lakes and houses as they neared the city. They rounded a curve in the highway and the sun lay directly in front of them, low in the sky. The man lowered the sun visor over the windshield. Richard shielded his eyes with his hand. The clock on the dash of the truck read twenty after five. Laura would be home by now. She would call his name and then wonder why he didn't respond. She would walk to the kitchen and look in the refrigerator. Then she'd go into the bedroom and rest her knapsack on the floor at the foot of the bed and look in his study. She'd examine his desk to see if he'd written anything that afternoon. He imagined her looking through the trash can. He realized then that she might find the crumpled page torn from his notebook. She would carry it to the bed, sit cross-legged with her running shoes still on, smoothing down the page on her thigh. Later he would walk in the door, covered in dust and dried sweat with burst blisters on his thumbs and the edge of his palm and she would not ask where he had gone or what he'd been doing.

"I found something odd in the trash today," she would say, after he came out of the shower and they sat down to dinner. She would ask him about it, out of curiosity, and he would not be able to explain. Or she might return the page to the wastebin, as if she had never found it, only bringing it up later, the next time they fought, using her discovery of his strange and morbid exercise as the very reason she finally decided to leave him.

Lloyd's neighbour took him as far as the apartment buildings. He pulled to a stop two blocks before the row houses began and left the engine running. Richard looked up the street, but the lemonade stand was gone. He stepped out of the cab into the warm evening air.

"Thanks for the lift," he said, and shut the door. The man touched the bill of his cap and then drove away.

June, 1978

"Have you tried getting him into one of those support groups?" said Joan. Lyle looked across the table at Susan and she could tell by his expression that he knew the answer didn't really matter.

"The woman's made up her mind, Joan," he said, almost yelling. "She's got to think about what's best for the girls."

Joan stood at the counter spooning coffee grounds into a chrome percolator.

"It's just the timing," said Joan. "If you could wait, hold out a little longer. Things might change. You know we won't be able to help you financially, now that Roy's starting college."

The phone rang in the living room and Joan put down the spoon and left them. Susan could hear the change in her sister's voice as she answered the phone. She took out a cigarette and reached in her purse for a lighter. Lyle placed his hand over hers. She looked at him and he looked directly back at her, without averting his gaze. His hand was dry and calloused and its weight pressed her bruised wrist painfully against the hard Formica of the table, though she tried not to let it show.

"Don't listen to her," he said. "You know best. We'll help you. You and the girls. However we can. I'll help you." Lyle was half deaf from the clamour of freight trains and tended to speak as if it was not himself who was hard of hearing but the person he addressed. There was a softness in his voice when he spoke to her alone. As soon as he had finished what he had to say he withdrew his hand from hers, picked up his coffee cup and lifted it halfway to his lips before he realized it was empty. He put it down and looked away and Susan took her lighter from her purse and lit her cigarette. She exhaled, careful to blow the smoke away from Lyle. They sat there for some time without speaking, the sound of Joan's voice in the other room filling the silence between them. Susan looked at her brother-in-law, sitting in the warm summer light. His hair had always been fair and thin and though she saw him only on occasion its gradual transition from blonde to white had been almost indiscernible. He was almost an old man she realized, fifteen years older than her own husband. He had recently developed a rasp when he breathed , which made him seem even older than fifty-three. Susan had heard such rasps at the hospital where she worked and knew the sickness they betrayed.

She stood up and put the lid on the percolator and plugged it in. Then she took a small carton of cream from the refrigerator and sat down.

"You've got your own to worry about," she said.

"You'd do the same," said Lyle. "Joan knows that too. She's just—unaccustomed. She doesn't handle these situations well."

The water began to percolate, lapping the glass-domed lid with a soft, erratic rhythm as the aroma of coffee filled the room.

"Lionel," said Susan, looking at him.

Joan hung up and came back into the kitchen, glanced at the table and went over to the breadbox.

"What kind of host are you, Lyle?" she said. "Would it

June, 1978

kill you?" She took out a lemon pound cake and put it on a plate, took a knife from a drawer and cut the cake into six slices.

"What did you two talk about?" she asked.

"I'd like for you to ship some things to me," said Susan. "After we find a place. I'll send you the money."

"You won't be gone that long, will you?" asked Joan. "I'm sure once he sees you mean business, that you won't put up with—"

"We'll send your things by rail," said Lyle. "We'll use my discount. It won't cost hardly anything."

Joan set the cake on the table along with three porcelain dessert plates.

"I still don't understand why you don't just stay with George and Edith in Grand Falls," said Joan.

Lyle turned to look at his wife. "Where is she going to work in Grand Falls?" He reached for a piece of cake and it crumbled in his hand, leaving a trail of crumbs between the plates.

"She won't need to work, Lyle, if she stays with George and Edith."

Lyle looked at Susan.

"Take the transfer. Find a home. Close to a school. You'll find a place. Joan and I have been talking about a trip to the coast for years now, haven't we Joan? I could use a vacation."

Joan filled their cups from the coffee pot and sat down on the chair between Susan and Lyle and looked at her sister.

"Lyle hasn't taken time off in years. Now that Roy's in college I figured I'd be going on vacation all by myself again this year."

Lyle sipped his coffee and looked at his wife.

"Susan came by with that casserole for me and Roy last year," he said, "while you were gone to Fort Lauderdale.

You remember that? Came by one evening on her way to work and dropped it off. You go away on vacation without me this year, I'm liable to starve to death."

Joan added two spoonfuls of sugar to her coffee, drew the last cigarette from Susan's pack, held it between her lips and lit it with Susan's lighter.

"Doctor says I need to take it easy," said Lyle. "Sea air would be good be for me. I figured I might take a couple of weeks this year. Did you tell Susan the good news, Joan?"

"What good news would that be, Lyle?" said Joan.

"Roy got a scholarship. Full tuition, and a stipend."

"That's wonderful," said Susan. "Smart kid."

Lyle looked at Susan.

"Smarter than his old man was," he said.

"You know what Roy told me the other day?" said Joan.

"When he came home from Jim's place?" She looked at Susan. "He said he was thinking about starting a band. Studying geography and he says he wants to play in a band. Bass guitar." She took a drag from her cigarette. "He gets these ideas sometimes."

Lyle cleared his throat. Joan looked at him.

"Did you know," she said, "that Herb used to be a singer, back when Sue first met him, before he started with the post office?"

"I knew that," said Lyle.

"What was the name of his group? That group he was in?" said Joan.

"The Dilettantes," said Susan.

Joan smiled.

"That was it," she said. "The Dilettantes. They never tried to go professional, did they?"

"No," said Susan. "I should get going."

"Already?" said Joan.

"I need to pick up the girls," said Susan.

June, 1978

"You still want that pattern?" said Joan. "For Sarah's communion dress?"

"I don't think I'll have the time," said Susan.

Joan stubbed her cigarette in the ashtray and stood up.

"I know exactly where it is. It won't take a minute," said Joan.

"That's not what I meant," said Susan.

"Of course you'll have time. It's not till next spring. I'll grab it." Joan went into the living room. "You want to take that cake home with you?" she called out. "Lyle doesn't eat it. And I shouldn't."

Susan reached for her purse on the table, but Lyle placed his hand upon the handle, picked it up as he pushed out his chair. He coughed as he stood up, his chest heaving, his face contorted with pain. With his free hand he reached toward his back pocket as if for a handkerchief, but it was a letter-sized envelope he produced, bulging slightly. Before Susan could protest he had opened the purse, slid the envelope inside, closed it and placed it in her hands.

"Things will work out," he said, softly. "You'll see. It always seems hardest just before you go through with it."

Aricia Agestis

The parasol over their table shielded the three of them from the late September sun. When Jacob saw the waiter eyeing their table, he beckoned for him. The waiter came over and cleared their plates away and filled Anna and David's coffee cups.

"Anything else?" he said.

"We're fine, thank you," said David.

"I would like a fruit cup," said Jacob. "A fruit cup and two grapefruit halves. Please."

"Very good," said the waiter. The waiter left and Anna leaned in toward Jacob.

"You're certain you weren't followed?" she said.

"Quite certain," said Jacob. "At least, not followed by anything with four legs."

"Well, that's all that matters, isn't it?" said Anna.

David stirred milk into his coffee and looked at Jacob.

"You look pale," he said. "When was the last time you left your apartment?"

"The day after I received the first acceptance letter," said Jacob. "From the *Mid-American Review*. A little over a month ago I suppose. That afternoon when I left my flat I noticed the Siamese that lives on the corner. Watching me."

"I know that Siamese," said Anna.

"She followed me to the library. I spent roughly two hours consulting the *Celtic Chieftain Compendium* and then when I emerged she was waiting for me. I walked home by a different route."

"But the Siamese was on to you," said David.

"You couldn't shake your tail," said Anna. David looked at Anna.

"Sorry," said Anna.

"You didn't, perhaps, fry up some tilapia for breakfast that day?" said David.

"Jacob doesn't eat fish," said Anna.

"I spent the rest of the day at home," said Jacob. "When I checked the mailbox the next morning there were two more acceptance letters."

"Jacob! Congratulations!" said Anna.

"Thank you," said Jacob.

"All that hard work of yours is finally paying off," said David. "Three acceptance letters."

"In two days," said Jacob.

"That's unprecedented," said David.

"Yes," said Jacob. "Normally I would have been elated. But when I left my apartment later that morning, the Siamese followed suit. By the time I reached the corner she had been joined by two companions. An obese, black cat with a white tuft at its neck, and a tabby. I recognized the tabby. Normally it wants nothing to do with the Siamese. But that day they were united by a common purpose."

"Tailing you," said Anna.

"When I got to the store I picked up the milk I needed and a lot of other things I hadn't intended on buying. I looked out the window before I left, and the coast was clear. But by the time I reached the corner, my entourage had reassembled. I would have tried to lose them, but I had weighed myself down with a five pound bag of potatoes. I glanced over my shoulder frequently. And there they were, the three of them. Lurking. Between fence posts and beneath parked cars. Never more than twenty feet behind."

The waiter arrived and set down a fruit cup and two grapefruit halves in front of Jacob.

"Thank you," said Jacob. The waiter nodded and left them. Jacob took up his spoon.

"And when you got home from the grocery store?" said David.

"I decided I would no longer leave my flat," said Jacob.

"For a whole month?" said David.

"But it's been so humid," said Anna.

"Stifling," said Jacob. "The warmest September in twenty-two years. I certainly thought about going outside. I became restless after the first few days. But then I received another acceptance letter."

"And you couldn't risk it," said David.

Anna placed her hand on David's.

"You know how Jacob feels about cats," she said.

"Yes," said David. "I know. Four separate acceptance letters."

"In the same week," said Jacob.

David took a sip of his coffee.

"David's been going through a bit of a dry spell," said Anna.

"What did you do up there all month?" said David.

"I kept writing," said Jacob. "Sending out submissions. One story a week."

"You're very brave," said Anna.

"But how did you mail them?" said David.

"The woman who lives below me," said Jacob. "With the accent. The Italian lawyer. Remember, David? The dark-haired woman."

"I remember," said David. "Go on."

"Her name is Sophia," said Jacob. "She took pity on me."

"You couldn't have told her," said David. "She wouldn't have believed you."

"I told her I was ill," said Jacob, "that I could barely make it down the stairs. The odd thing was that after I spoke to her, I did feel a bit feverish, slightly delirious. I've felt that way ever since. Sophia was very compassionate. Sometimes the people you least expect, who seem indifferent to you otherwise, can surprise you."

"She mailed your submissions," said Anna.

"I would leave them in her mail slot," said Jacob. "Early Monday morning. She would drop them in the mailbox at the end of the street on her way to work." He ate a spoonful of his fruit cup.

"How do you know she mailed them?" said David.

"I would watch her from my front window," said Jacob.

"Would she bring you groceries?" said Anna.

"Several times a week," said Jacob. "Chicken soup mostly. And Sicilian fig pastries. Whenever I saw her I would put in a request for fresh fruit. But she could never seem to remember."

"How do you know it was your submissions she was mailing?" said David. "If you left them in her mail slot, you can't be sure."

"Why wouldn't she mail them?" said Anna.

"Hmm," said Jacob. "I'm afraid David does have a point. Theoretically, she might have switched the envelopes. Perhaps she kept my stories for herself, revised them, even. Sent them out pseudonymously. It is possible. But what you have to understand is that my most recent material is rather unconventional. Highly fantastical, characterised by a good deal of looming menace, these stories I've been writing. I can't imagine someone reading these stories and not evincing some sort of a tell-tale response, giving themselves away when they delivered my fig pastries and chicken soup."

"Lawyers are good bluffers," said David. "It comes with the territory."

"No doubt," said Jacob.

A slight breeze ruffled the napkins on the table. Jacob noticed that the sky had darkened considerably. He took a last spoonful of cantaloupe from his fruit cup before moving onto the grapefruit. As he ate he looked at goose bumps forming on Anna's downy arms. She shivered, a pouting expression on her lips.

"There's something I don't understand," she said. "When you woke up this morning, how did you know the cats wouldn't follow you anymore?"

"An excellent question," said Jacob. "All I can tell you is that it has to do with the dream."

"Yes?" said Anna. She looked at Jacob expectantly.

"But I shouldn't get ahead of myself," said Jacob. "Before I tell you about the dream you must know that yesterday, for the first time since May, since graduation, I was unable to write."

"Happens to the best of us," said David.

"It used to happen to me all the time," said Jacob. "More often than not I would be entirely blocked. I used to come to you for advice."

"I remember," said David.

Anna crossed her bare legs and smiled at Jacob.

"But then you found your stride," she said.

"I spent last week working on a new story," said Jacob. "But by the weekend I was desperately behind schedule. I couldn't seem to figure out an ending without repeating myself. Nothing worked. I couldn't get anywhere. It's a miserable feeling."

"You've reached the end of your creative cycle," said David.

"That occurred to me," said Jacob. "But it didn't make me feel any better. Eventually I gave up and went to bed."

David looked away and Jacob followed his gaze to a tall, thin woman with a heart-shaped face seated alone on the far corner of the patio.

"You had this dream," said David.

"I couldn't sleep at first," said Jacob. "And when I finally did I dreamt of two little English girls in frilly summer dresses and knee-high stockings."

"Are you sure you want to tell us about this dream?" said David.

"How old were the girls?" said Anna.

"One was about nine or ten years old. The dark haired one. The other one was younger, with flaxen hair, but I didn't know that at first because she was holding me in her lap."

"Oh," said Anna.

"I think we've heard enough," said David.

"David," said Jacob, "You know me better than that. It wasn't that kind of dream. You see, I wasn't human."

"What were you?" said Anna.

"A kitten," said Jacob.

"Cute," said David.

"We were all on a gingham blanket on a cliff overlooking the sea. There was a wicker picnic basket and the dark haired girl took out a miniature porcelain tea service and they had tea and soda crackers," said Jacob.

"Too young for tea," said David.

"It was a dream, David," said Anna.

"No, you're right," said Jacob. "It was apple juice in the teapot I think, and a saucer of milk for me."

"How thoughtful," said Anna.

"I couldn't resist," said Jacob. "I squirmed out of flaxen hair's grasp and lapped up the milk as if it were the best thing I'd ever tasted. And the girls spoke to one another."

"What did they say?" asked Anna.

"You know, it's funny," said Jacob. "I usually don't remember anything about my dreams. But I recall this one so vividly. The dark haired one said, 'He really must cease these tiresome short stories.'"

"Come on," said David.

"What did the blonde one say?" said Anna.

"She said, 'They are getting rather repetitious, aren't they?' And then the dark hair said, 'Quite.'"

Anna laughed with delight. She reached over and hit Jacob gently in the arm with the back of her hand.

"They didn't really talk like that," said David, "like characters in a Victorian novel. Lewis Carroll."

"Why not?" said Anna.

"Here's where it gets interesting," said Jacob. "By that point I had finished the milk and I lay there on the blanket in the sun, looking up at them sipping their apple juice. And dark hair said, 'It's high time he attempted a novel,' and then, 'It better be a good one too, for we both know what must come to pass upon its completion.'" Jacob paused for a mouthful of grapefruit. David looked at his watch.

"Then flaxen hair suddenly looked very solemn," said Jacob. "And she reached over to where I lay in the grass and she picked me up and placed me in her lap."

"I'll bet she did," said David.

"David," said Anna.

"She looked at the dark-haired girl," said Jacob, "and she stroked me between the ears and said, 'Surely kittens would survive?' And dark hair, without skipping a beat, she set her teacup down on her saucer and said, 'Not even kittens. And besides, there would be no one left to cuddle them, or change their kitty litter, and if there was any milk for them to drink, it would surely be radioactive.'"

"Huh," said Anna.

"That's the last thing I heard them say," said Jacob. "Because right after that a butterfly fluttered dangerously close to the edge of the blanket."

"A monarch butterfly?" said David.

"A Brown Argus," said Jacob, " known to lepidopterists as *Aricia Agestis*. Recognizable by the white fringe and orange markings on the top of its brown wings.

"Impressive," said David.

"I wasn't able to control myself," said Jacob. "I leaped out of the little girl's lap and caught its wing with the tiny claws of my right paw, and then sank my kitten-fangs into its thorax. Then flaxen hair screamed and I woke up."

"I don't buy it," said David. "How did you recognize the butterfly?"

"The last time I saw Sophia—" said Jacob.

"What has she got to do with this?" said David.

"Sophia knows I like to read," said Jacob. "The last time I saw her she took it upon herself to provide a book, along with my rations. A 1977 edition of *Flatman's and Alfin's Field Guide to the Butterflies of Western Europe*."

David raised an eyebrow.

"Your guess is as good as mine," said Jacob. "At any rate, it helped me fall asleep."

"And this morning?" said Anna.

"This morning, despite having slept for no more than three hours, I woke up at dawn, entirely refreshed, knowing three things with absolute certainty."

"Which were?" said Anna.

"First, that my fever, which I believe to be psychosomatic—a kind of self-imposed penance for my fib to Sophia—had finally broken. Second, that one unlikely epoch had come to its conclusion and another had begun. In other words, that I could make a breakfast date with my closest friends, whom I had not seen for far too long, that I could come to this café and sit on its patio entirely without fear of feline menace. I happened to pass the tabby on my way here, as a matter of fact, and he just lay there on the sidewalk, sunning himself, unmoving, indifferent to my presence."

"And third?" said Anna.

"Third," said Jacob, "that the strangely bitter taste in my mouth was one of the most unpleasant sensations in recent memory, and had to be dealt with immediately."

"What a story," said David.

"Well done," said Anna.

"Thank you," said Jacob.

David took a sip of coffee.

"Hold on a minute," he said. "I'm not saying I buy any of this. You're a very imaginative guy, Jacob, we all know that."

Anna looked at David and David looked Jacob in the eye.

"Let's just say I'm willing to play along," said David.

"I'm all ears," said Jacob.

"Let's say," said David, "for the sake of argument, let's say there's some kind of correlation between your publications and the behaviour of the neighbourhood cats."

"Let's," said Jacob.

"And that the little girls in the dream," said David, "the nymphets, have something to do with this correlation."

"What are you getting at, David?" said Anna.

"I'm suggesting," said David, "that the fact Jacob arrived here today, unaccompanied, isn't all that comforting."

In the periphery of his vision, Jacob noticed the waiter eying their table. Anna frowned at David.

"I don't understand," she said. "In the dream Jacob was a

cat. He confronted his fear."

"Yes," said David. "Good for Jacob. But I'm talking about what the little girls said. About Jacob writing a novel and the end of the world."

"Assuming the girls were talking about me," said Jacob.

"Who else would they be talking about?" said David. "It was your dream."

"In that case," said Jacob, "this is a very serious concern." He looked toward the darkening horizon. Cumulonimbus clouds had entirely obscured the sun.

"Let me ask you something, Jacob," said David.

"Of course," said Jacob.

"Why do you write?"

Jacob stared down at his plate and placed one grapefruit rind on top of the other, so as to make a whole, deflated grapefruit, sitting in a puddle of grapefruit juice.

"Because I suppose it's the only thing I know how to do," he said. "I used to believe what we were taught in our seminars, that I was serving some important moral purpose, trying to teach myself the proper way to live. But the last few weeks have tested my sanity."

Anna placed her hand on David's. She looked at Jacob.

"So what are you going to do?" she asked.

David withdrew his hand and flagged the waiter.

"He has to make a choice."

* * *

Jacob was soaked to the skin by the time he returned to his flat. He took off his wet clothes and hung them in the bathroom and brushed his teeth. Then he flossed and rinsed with antiseptic mouthwash, the bitter taste still lingering in his mouth. He stood in front of the mirror, gazing at his reflection. He hardly recognized himself. His cheeks were sunken and his nose appeared more aquiline than ever before. His complexion, which had always been pallid, was now almost ghostly and the contrast with his raven-hair and freckles was startling. He left the bathroom and picked up a t-shirt and a pair of jeans from the floor, sniffed them and then pulled them on and sat at his desk. He looked out the window at the street below. Sodden oak leaves drifted in puddles and collected in gutters. He had planned a trip to the laundromat that afternoon but the rain showed no sign of letting up.

His ancient Smith-Corona rested on the desk before him, safely beneath its matte black cover. It occurred to him, that unlike his previous neighbours, Sophia had never complained about the noise of his typewriter. He decided he should give her a thank-you gift, a fruit basket, when he returned her book. Perhaps she would be touched by his gratitude and invite him into her apartment. But he thought this unlikely. He thought of Anna in the morning sunlight, recalled the way she looked at him when she listened to him speak, holding her coffee cup in both hands, her lips pursed. He thought of David's analytical mind, how it had impressed him when they had met the year before in their modernism seminar. He thought of the night he had first introduced David to Anna, and how the two of them had been inseparable ever since.

Then the idea came to him. He got up and walked away from his desk and by the time he had paced the length of the room three times the idea could no longer be contained within the confines of a short story. It was a narrative unlike any he had previously conceived, one that could only be adequately expressed through copious detail and characterization, comprised of events that spanned considerable distances in space and in time. Sentences and chapter outlines composed themselves in his head. But he could not bring himself to put them on paper. A moral impulse quelled his writer's instinct. He was left with nothing to do but heat a can of chicken soup and wait for the rain to let up.

* * *

The rain did not subside until late the next morning. Jacob had two Sicilian fig pastries for breakfast before dragging his soiled clothing to the laundromat. As he thumbed through an old *National Geographic* and listened to the rotations of the double-load dryer, the novel continued to compose itself in his head. By the time he returned home the pavement had dried and the afternoon shadows had begun to grow. He changed into clean clothes, put away his laundry, and descended the stairs once again. As he walked the six blocks from his flat to the grocery store he passed two little girls in t-shirts and jeans playing hop scotch on the sidewalk. They sang a nonsense song as he passed by and eyed him warily.

He took his time in the grocery store and found satisfaction in remembering precisely the items he required: a loaf of bread, a dozen eggs, six oranges, four grapefruits, four limes, a can of beans, a package of frozen peas. It was not until the walk home that his mind began to wander and he found himself immersed once again in the environs of his unwritten novel. It was dusk by this time and when he rounded the corner he did not notice the tail of the Siamese as it flitted beneath his feet. But he heard the feline shriek and the hiss that followed and he felt the pain as the claw penetrated his sock and grazed the flesh of his ankle. The over-filled paper bag slipped from his grasp. Citrus fruit bombarded the sidewalk and rolled in every direction. He glared at the Siamese as it retreated beneath the underside of the nearest stoop. Then he looked down at the dented can and the upside down egg carton at his feet, resting in a puddle of translucent ooze.

He stooped to gather the salvageable groceries into the damp bag and continued on his way. As he crossed the street he looked back and saw the silhouette of the Siamese emerge to lap the egg from the sidewalk.

The pain in his ankle had not subsided by the time he reached his flat. He dumped his groceries on the counter without bothering to put them away. He went to the bathroom and from the medicine cabinet he took a bottle of peroxide and liberally daubed his ankle. Then he sat himself at his desk, removed the cover from his typewriter and began to write in earnest.

Acknowledgements

The author wishes to express his gratitude to Robbie MacGregor, Nic Boshart, Terence Byrnes, Matthew Kennedy, Rob Sternberg, Katherine Kline, Kelly Code-McNeil and John McNeil, Burgandy Code and Ryan Rogerson, Erin Code and Gorden Videen, Larissa Muzzy, Caleb Latreille, Jeff Miller and the Soul Gazers, Jane Buss and the Writers' Federation of Nova Scotia, Mary di Michele, John Steffler, Megan Fildes, Marianne and John Scandiffio, and specially to Carolyn.

Invisible Publishing is committed to working with writers who might not ordinarily be published and distributed commercially. We work exclusively with emerging and under-published authors to produce entertaining, affordable, print-based art.

We believe that books are meant to be enjoyed by everyone and that sharing our stories is important. In an effort to ensure that books never become a luxury, we do all that we can to make our books more accessible.

We are collectively organized, our production processes are transparent. At Invisible, publishers and authors recognize a commitment to one another, and to the development of communities which can sustain and encourage storytellers.

If you'd like to know more please get in touch
info@invisiblepublishing.com

Invisible Publishing
Halifax & Montréal

MEMBER OF SCABRINI GROUP

Québec, Canada
2007